More praise for Spent Sc

"Smith rocks and rolls with his tales of music, booze, drugs, and bicycle racing. This book has it all."

> — **BONNIE JO CAMPBELL**, author of *Mothers, Tell Your Daughters & Other Stories, Once Upon a River*, and *American Salvage*

"Spent Saints plays the minor chords of tragedy and the power ballads of redemption with skilled and steady hands. These heartsick, clear-eyed stories celebrate the will to love and live better at every turn."

> — **JOHN EVANS**, author of *Should I Still Wish, Young Widower* and *The Consolations*

"We cannot imagine the pain that is headed our way. We can only guess at the precise contours of the hells we are about to inflict upon ourselves. Chained to our own rocks, ringed by electric fences we have built inside our minds, we can scarcely comprehend that all we have to do is walk away. Oh, yes. In these knife-edged, fiercely intelligent stories, Brian Smith tells us all about these truths, his characters delivering to us hard-won knowledge that is both terrifying and oddly exhilarating, like walking down the streets of a bad neighborhood at midnight. Read them, reflect on them, admire them — then drink a glass of orange juice and get yourself to the gym."

> — **GREGORY McNAMEE**, author of *Gila* and *Blue Mountains Far Away*

First Ridgeway Press edition 2017
©2017 Brian Jabas Smith

The Ridgeway Press
P.O. Box 120
Roseville, Michigan, 48066
USA
www.ridgewaypress.org

Book design by Dennis Rhodes, www.flammablecreations.com
Cover and author photo by Moose Azim, www.mooseazim.com
Interior photos by Brian Smith
Cover model: Tulah Smith

Publisher's Cataloging-in-Publication data:

Names: Smith, Brian Jabas, author.

Title: Spent saints & other stories / Brian Jabas Smith.

Description: Detroit, MI: Ridgeway Press, 2017.

Identifiers: ISBN 978-1-56439-008-0 | LCCN 2016945959

Subjects: LCSH Substance abuse--Fiction. | Drug addiction--Fiction. | Alcoholism--Fiction. | Methamphetamine--Fiction. | Man-woman relationships--Fiction. | BISAC FICTION/General.

Classification: LCC PS3619.M5536 S64 2017 | DDC 813.6--dc23

Printed in the United States of America
10 9 8 7 6 5 4 3 2

Earlier versions of the following stories have been published here: "Spent Saints" (*Antonin Artaud Publications*), "The Delivery Man" (Detroit *Metro Times*), "Lost in the Supermarket" (*Literary Orphans*).

This is a work of fiction. Names, places and scenes are either a product of the author's invention or used fictitiously.

SPENT SAINTS

& other stories

Brian Jabas Smith

Table of Contents

Lost
in the
Supermarket

Lost in the Supermarket

Rowdy swore it was piss. Hot streams splashed him in intervals, and he counted, six seconds on, 15 seconds off. One arm had numbed under him and the underside of the other burned. A side of his face burned too, and he squeezed his eyes tighter.

He heard a lawnmower fire up but he was a long ways from it and he drifted back to summer between fifth and sixth grade. That time Mike Zimmers and his three little Stingray-mounted disciples crashed him and his bike into the arroyo in the desert behind his house. They unzipped and let him have it, right there in the 105-degree twilight and when they finished they shook their dicks for a long while down close to his face. Zimmers got hard.

A car door slammed and its engine revved once into a smooth idle. *German made.* Rowdy imagined himself behind the wheel, air-conditioned sober ease in a new suit and fresh coffee in hand, heading out to work in a smoked-glass high-rise over the parkway. An office that smelled of new carpeting and featured a panoramic view that took in Sky Harbor International and Camelback Mountain. That'd be the shit, an office like that.

Another engine sparked into hum. An SUV.

Rowdy thought of his wife. *It's been a year.* They used to

drink wine and beer and sometimes whiskey and get all hot and fuck for hours. Their friends would often ask what's that glow on their faces. Then one day she got the dream job, with responsibilities and an adult wage. He'd stayed on with the drywall contractors because a ton of new construction in greater Phoenix meant steady work. They moved into a bi-level over west of 35th Avenue, thinking maybe they'd rent awhile and then buy when their credit improved. Things were pretty good for a change. He'd finally landed on the other side of life.

Rowdy opened his eyes to a squint and the sun unloaded inside his skull. He lifted a hand to shade the punishment, and flashes of life refracted off wet blades of grass in front of his face, a blanched suburban landscape behind that.

He coughed and slowly rolled over and upright into a sitting position and a whole world flipped right side up. Flawless symmetries of houses and yards repeated one end off the other and disappeared blocks away over the far side of a hill. Boom-roomy tract houses with polished door hinges and wagon-wheel mailboxes and shiny cars that left no oil stains on driveways, each home filled with a happy family so perfect that they left no mark in front yards or on the street, never an errant playground toy or uncoiled garden hose. The sprayed-on stucco and rectangle swathes of green against sharp desert landscape showed no connection between what was old and what was new, no nods to previous cultures, worlds, existences. It just was.

His hangover made things blur and shift and boxy pastel missions became clapboard colonials became prop-up Victorians. Each yard seemed like a tally of Home Depot bills, some developer's idea of a garden of Allah in a desert that for thousands of years hadn't changed but in less than three years had been manhandled into water-greedy lawn dreams and LED-lighted water fountains and butterfly-winged plants hauled in from faraway lands like Ohio and Pennsylvania that had yet to brown and die. Brand-newness owned everything, like the hundreds of homes he'd worked on. Rowdy saw it all as unreachable success, the kind of success designed for people who aren't him.

He turned his head to look in the opposite direction and saw the same except for a dividing intersection and a distant golf course carved into a rocky hillside. Why would anyone stick a golf course where there never should be one? He reminded himself that people do what they must to survive. He understood a need to survive, how it manifests into a profound blankness that's a long long way from ever returning to nature. People here overcame the odds to live and breathe on these streets and lead dreamed-of lives with their wives and their wounds and their kids.

Ain't such a bad way to go.

Clean, rinsed suburbia always made Rowdy aware and ashamed of his scars, and he felt like a dirty outsider. He longed for that car, that dog, that wife, that dental plan, that stainless-steel refrigerator stocked to the gills. He could be unsoiled, walled in by all-you-can-drink wet bars and swimming pools, with big screens in every room and fake Mexican tiles and giant silk pillows on king-sized beds. Everything would be swollen — the cars, the faces, the lawns, the sun, the wallets, the sky, the produce sections, the cancer, the lives. He wanted to be numbed and comforted by all of that safety, diversion, excess.

The dreaming stopped when Rowdy realized that he'd come to on someone's trimmed triangle of mowed grass, soaking in sprinkler water. His lips were cracked and his mouth tasted like cat shit. A woman stood in the living-room window, thick arms, mom hair, scowling face.

Aw, fuck.

He pulled himself up and shuffle-walked toward the sidewalk. South Mountain was hazy in the distance and that meant he was somewhere in North Phoenix, north of Thunderbird Avenue, and a long ways from his shitty apartment off Van Buren. He moved up the sidewalk toward the rise in the street.

The new house and her new job had meant the drinking and the frolic would suffer, and it did. They stopped touching each other. Rowdy figured things would've fixed themselves if only he'd slowed his drinking. He promised to go cold turkey. So he switched from everyday drinking to "only on weekends." His weekday sobriety stretched out to two months and he was surprised at how long he tolerated himself as his personal disciplinarian. He pitched in more with the chores too, the dishes, the laundry. He'd taken up running. He did anything he could to combat the breakdown that was beginning to suffocate their home, where laughter and music and conversation and sex and food and movies had once created an impenetrable bubble of domestic bliss, where mornings burst with possibility and nights wound down on gentle gestures of warmth and love.

But things only continued to head south. He'd go to work, and so would she. He'd come home and drink too many beers and she'd make supper and then they'd watch their TV shows in bed and she'd doze off. The next morning they'd wake up and hit repeat. Rowdy never did learn to converse like a grown-up, much less stay calm when things went bad. Instead, he'd clam up and pray for sunny outcomes or shout mean, hateful shit. He'd never hit her. No, he could never do that. He'd learned from the best.

A hot breeze smelling of swimming pools rustled his hair and the hint of chlorine got him. He stopped, teetered, and placed his hands on his knees. A squat, sweat-soaked guy was mowing his lawn wearing only bike shorts and Rowdy's insides roiled. Dear god, no … He felt it come up. Oh, god … The most foul booze-y swill surged up and splashed the sidewalk between his stupid black boots and decorated his lower pant legs. The street dived, nearly pulled him headfirst into his own sickness. He heaved a second time.

A silver SUV rolled by, a mom with three young kids in the back. Rowdy might as well have been a bloody carcass dangling from a mangled car that had screeched into a telephone pole at 60 miles per hour, because that's how he felt when those kids glared at him. Their expressions shifted from happy-playful to little-kid versions of the what-the-fuck look, wrinkled brows and curled lips. He now scared kids.

SUV Mom sped up when she passed. Maybe she called the cops? He dragged his forearm across his mouth, wiped it on his pant leg, straightened up and continued down the street. Sweat ran down his back, legs and face. But he felt a little better.

———

The worse he'd feel the better his wife would look. And she was hot to begin with: Sexy-smart, a fan of books, and curvy with a stop-traffic ass.

She'd started to make calls at night and step out to the backyard for privacy. He'd taken to watching through a window where the blinds were pulled down, and she'd occasionally look up at it to see if he was spying. She'd talk and pace and smoke and laugh a lot, and sometimes lean against the tree and look down at her feet and talk quietly with a big grin on her face, and would have that dreamy look of wonder like it had when she and Rowdy first connected.

When the phone calls would end she'd step back in through the back door all happy, but Rowdy could see how she'd deflate at the sight of him but pretend not to. His efforts to smile and accept that maybe that kind of arms-length detachment was good enough to sustain a marriage only hurt more. She'd never said a word about those 45-minute phone conversations, until he'd worked up the nerve to ask.

"It was nobody. Work stuff." Then she'd head off to mix a drink and then to the computer and that would be that.

One day he walked in the front door after 11 hours of hanging drywall in the ugliest, hammered-together suburban skeletons anyone can imagine and someone had obviously backed a moving van up to their front door, loaded it up and took off. Looked like someone had turned the house upside down and then put it right again, only leaving his remaining things where they fell. Books and records and wall hangings and drawers and all their shit scattered everywhere, and holes in walls showed that furniture had been removed in haste, and dust rats and magazines and kitchen things. Their terrified girl cat Otis was hiding in a crawlspace behind the water heater.

First, Rowdy hyperventilated. Then rose a scream that started in his toes and blossomed straight up through his body and out his mouth, but was dead silent. She'd left him, hard.

Only her things were gone, mostly. The antique Victorian chaise and matching chairs, and that strange silver giraffe (she loved giraffes) whose home was atop the mantle, and the Flannery O'Conner first editions and Bessie Smith and New

York Dolls albums. Rowdy loved that she'd play Smith and The Dolls back-to-back after her second drink of the night. It made her so happy. But he'd stomped out that happiness. It had gotten to the point that whenever she was happy it had nothing to do with him. And there was nothing he could do.

The closets held nothing more than his ugly, washed-too-many-times shirts that'd she'd so often hang there after doing their laundry, and his crappy coats misaligned on flimsy hangers.

Things she'd left stung the most, like the framed picture of them on the steps of his grandma's house in Idaho. Grandma snapped that and two weeks later she was dead. She'd left things he'd bought her on birthdays and anniversaries, or to show that he'd been trying, books, lamps, a rug. He couldn't look at things she'd given him, slightly imperfect gifts chosen with the purest of intentions and filled with promises that she would never, under any circumstances, live without him.

Rowdy was beginning to feel like he was the star of his own cartoon and the outdoor scene was a wraparound backdrop that repeated every three houses or so, again and again.

Two boys on mountain bikes began riding circles in the street beside him. One had skinny legs and unkempt hair and wore a black Pantera tour T-shirt; the other was freckle-cheeked and fat with bushy red hair. They looked about 14 and wore baggy shorts. Rowdy felt sorry for the fat one.

They split wide to let a German car power by. Its driver was scooting up in his seat as he passed. He wore a tie. The skinny kid waved at the driver. Rowdy watched the car pass and knew in that moment the driver's version of normal absolutely blew away his own version of normal, and he wished he could go back and undo every fucked up thing he ever did.

Rowdy was "never intact," his wife would say. Oh, he may have been there physically. Even before things had worsened until they were never good, he'd already been feeling like he had to suffer and pay. Besides having to resume the meetings (he'd hate himself more if he didn't do the meetings), he had to push to be honest and that shit was hardly second nature. He had to relearn how to fake happiness like he did when he was a kid, even when there wasn't one goddamned thing to look forward to. Like after the time his scoutmaster had his pants off and things turned ugly.

Rowdy maintained a faltering gait on the sidewalk. To stop thinking of his ex-wife he pressed hard to recall the previous night. One thing for certain was that he'd consumed mad amounts of alcoholic beverages. That was fact because he'd been hitting the bottle each and every night until angels appeared. That's just what he did now.

He remembered walking into the Emerald Lounge on 7th Avenue, meeting Shelly there. She then drove to the golf course way out past Sunnyslope, beyond Thunderbird Road, with a bottle of Southern Comfort and 12-pack that they'd purchased at some liquor store along the way. The golf course was graveyard quiet and they stretched out together beneath all those stars, chasing the beer with the Southern Comfort. Shelly was cool with her cowboy boots and big sad eyes and never-ending embraces. He'd known Shelly since before he got married and she obviously knew something was wrong with him because she always told him that everything would be all right, as if she really believed it herself.

Rowdy glanced over his shoulder and saw that the two teens

were still pedaling in circles beside him. Shouldn't the little fuckers be in school or something? The thought prompted Rowdy to rifle his pant pockets, where he found the brass loop with his three keys (car, mailbox, and front door), and four wadded up dollar bills. He never carried a wallet because he'd never replaced the last one he'd lost. It was the same deal with a cellphone. But four dollars felt like riches. That's how it was now: Four dollars. That was for beer and a phone call once he happened upon a convenience store.

The skinny kid pulled up next to Rowdy and rolled along. The kid looked at Rowdy, up-nodded once, and said, "What's with you, dude? Lost?"

Rowdy formed a weak smile. He was too tired for hassles and felt a heatstroke or something coming on. He said, "Yep. Pretty normal for me."

The kid spun a few bike lengths ahead and pulled a wheelie. Then he flipped around and pedaled toward Rowdy and said, in all seriousness, as he was passing, "Too bad for you, dude." Rowdy watched him roll back around and rejoin the fat kid. The two bumped knuckles and steered a big circle in the street, going a little faster than before, leaning in harder, the skinny kid leading the fat one. No matter how tough those pubescent turds thought they were, Rowdy thought, or how tough they supposed they could one day be, they couldn't shake that strangely healthy-happy look of factory-made kids from the suburbs, with their big feet in overpriced kicks, and all the hyper energy needed to jump curbs and pull 20-second wheelies. The overall affect of boyhood menace is silly when it hasn't been grown into yet, when little convicts are just festering inside.

Rowdy made it up over the rise and saw where the subdivision ended and the desert began. It was only four houses away. He spotted the tall sign of a Circle K rise above the large patch of desert and that was his refuge. Felt like a wild rock pigeon heading for home. He could make it for sure, and he'd get refreshed, figure out where the hell he was. He'd payphone his pal Jerry for a lift back downtown. Jerry didn't do much so Rowdy knew he'd be home. Jerry was a pretty damn good friend. He'd have beer and shade while waiting for Jerry's air-conditioned truck to pick him up. Then he'd be home, ready for the night to come down. Rowdy always looked forward to the nights. As long as night was coming he had something to count on.

If Jerry weren't home, he'd call Shelly, if he could remember her phone number. He wasn't sure what their status was after the previous night because all he could remember were those stars. How he wound up on that woman's lawn was a mystery.

Rowdy stepped into the desert and was relieved to be off the street. His stomach had relaxed some, but the sun was really laying into him. He stopped in the shade under a mesquite tree and used the bottom of his shirt to wipe the sweat off his face and out of his eyes. He told himself he'd rest a long minute before making the final couple-hundred-yard slog to the store.

The two kids rolled up in the dirt and stopped a few feet behind him.

Why the hell were they still following him? He spun around and saw the fat kid first, a sweaty blob with a balloon head and a ruddy uneasy look. The skinny kid looked corrupt and full of juvenile detention-room rage. He pushed his bike to the ground, picked up a rock, and stepped toward Rowdy. The rock was spherical, strange for this part of desert, Rowdy thought, three times the size of the kid's fist, practically a boulder. The kid licked sweat off his top lip.

Rowdy thought of the note his wife had left for him on the

day she'd moved out. It said: I couldn't stand by and watch the light fade out of you. She'd told him once that he was dying faster than anyone she'd ever met and that his mere presence alone could never right any kind of a wrong. He could never just be. He longed for her.

The kid shifted and the rock came at Rowdy's face and the desert heat buzzed, and the electrical wires that arched between giant transmission towers buzzed, and he could hear the air conditioners hum and the swimming pool filters hum, and it all looped together into a strangely hypnotic suburban aria, safety and comfort sizzling everywhere.

The
Grand Prix

The Grand Prix

His foot clipped into the pedal and the pedal was connected to the crank and his leg pushed down and perspiration stung razor burns on the tops of his shins. His 17-pound, custom-made, salmon pink Andy Gilmour hummed beneath him. It was warm out, overcast and murky.

After a few warm-up miles and many stoplights, he spun back around and headed to the team van, where Freddie Z. stood waiting for him. Julian unclipped from his right pedal, rolled to a stop and looked up at his coach, who was holding out a water bottle and a towel draped over his forearm.

"Julian," Freddie grinned, "You look ready."

Julian took the water bottle, drank from it, and placed it in the holder on his bike. "Just water and sodium," Freddie said. "That's all you need for today."

Julian nodded and used the towel to wipe sweat from his face.

When Julian first met Freddie Z., he thought the coach was just some giant Ukrainian with a mean face who maybe beat people up for a living or loaded trucks. He had a blocky jaw and a big red nose. Julian learned quickly that Freddie not only offered keen insights into advanced methods of sports medicine and science but he'd already nurtured more than a dozen

Eastern Bloc cyclists to Olympic gold medals and lucrative professional cycling careers.

Freddie stared straight into Julian's eyes and said, "Remember, this race is not important."

But it is, Julian thought.

To Freddie, Julian was more than just a teenager with an inexplicable shortage of self-confidence. He was a kid who had little understanding of who he was and who he was going to be. He was just learning to navigate adolescence, one weighed down heavily, and quite importantly for any future world champion, Freddie thought, by his 24-hour-a-day obsession with bike racing. Freddie, of course, wouldn't waste his time on any cyclist who didn't show a will, no, an actual desire, to suffer extremities, to live and die on the bike like a madman. Most riders, even the good ones, didn't possess that will, nor did they expect to come up against it in someone else. Freddie saw in Julian potential world domination. Freddie's concern was Julian's low self-esteem. It played against type.

Freddie continued. "Julian, you are going to be a huge cycling star." Freddie had been telling Julian that for more than a year now, since naming him, at 14, to the U.S. Junior National Team, a spot reserved for a few elite national cyclists under the age of 18. He added, "Don't forget that."

Because Freddie's command of English wasn't too good, he'd often relay what Julian interpreted as sincere instruction mostly through eye contact, which was stealth-like. Once his dark eyes connected to Julian's there was no escaping them.

"Just stay to front of the field for safety," Freddie said. "It's very dangerous today. Do your best in sprint, and stay away from crashes. Tomorrow is Nest Mountain race. You go for that win tomorrow." He felt Freddie's huge calloused hand come to rest on his back. The hand felt like it belonged to someone's dad, and it comforted him. "This today you need for experience." Julian believed his every word.

The bicycle race and the Long Beach Grand Prix Formula One event were each held on the exact same freeway and streets, on the same day, the difference was the bike racecourse was shorted to a one-mile circuit, from its nearly two-mile route used for the autos. The cyclists were to race 65 laps in the evening after the Formula One.

Julian had no teammates his age because there wasn't anyone else in the race under 18. Because he was on the U.S. Junior National Team he was accepted to race among the older guys, the Category One racers and pros, a field limited to 100 of the classiest in the United States. But because Julian was a junior, he had a gear restriction, meaning he couldn't use the giant gears the others had when the race got fast. He'd have to pedal faster to maintain speed, a big handicap on a flat course in a fast race. Julian had to stay in the slipstream of others to even have a chance, staying an inch behind the wheel in front of him. (Slipstreaming offers a slight sensation that you're being pulled along, and can save a third of a racer's energy).

Julian knew many of the adult-age National Team guys from the Olympic Training Center in Colorado Springs, where he lived on and off in the dorms there. Those guys hailed from far-off lands like Wisconsin and Florida and California and Vermont, and they stressed uniformity, had the same arrogance and everything seemed to come easy to them. They laughed at the same jokes, wore the same clothes, saw the same movies, listened to the same music, had the same haircut. The world was designed for them. They scared him.

They'd taken to calling him Dickweed because he listened to stuff like Johnny Thunders and cut his own hair into a fuckedup spiky mess. He was forced to listen to his blaster after his Walkman had died — on The Clash's "Death or Glory" — and that's when he discovered punk rock rankled the big, tough, world-class racers in the dorms, even at low volume in the middle of the day with doors closed. Julian never understood enmity from other cyclists; especially those who understood the suffering this sport required. Why make it worse, Julian wondered, on a fellow National Team member?

After Dickweed began dropping those older guys in the mountains outside of Colorado Springs, they regarded him with a kind of gape-jawed contempt and lobbied to have him tossed out of the OTC.

Julian left his coach and hit the racecourse to warm up. The crowds that hadn't dispersed looking for over-priced hot dogs and beer sat bored or drunk in temporary stands erected along waterfront streets. Palm trees and glass buildings rose behind concrete blockades and tall chain link fences topped with barbed wire.

The race circuit began on a flat section of closed-off freeway. Two right-hand hairpins, each decreasing in radius, followed slightly curved straightaways including four lanes of Shoreline Drive, and the six-lane freeway, whose midpoint was the start/finish line.

These streets were not his streets in his desert town. These streets smelled mainly of Formula One roadkill and racecar excrement — seared fiberglass and rotisserie meat, and motor oil, pit stops and armpits. Crash soot on freeway walls looked like big calla lilies.

The race organizers didn't clean the course too well after earlier racecar crashes, which spewed oil and gasoline everywhere. Bike racers called these long oily slicks "invisible death," and the little dome dividers between lanes were even more deadly from it. If you happened to clip one, forget it, your front wheel would skitter out from under you, a dozen riders would slam into you and asphalt would sear thighs, torsos and faces. Scarred for life.

Julian watched bike-racing stars from dreamland burbs like Menlo Park or Newport Beach or Los Altos pull up in Volvos and Audis. The surfer-blond untouchables with perfect skin, concrete bodies and celebrity grins, who grew up admired by others and enjoyed parents who supported them through teen cycling years with money and love, invested time and energy, and the best pro racing bikes and coaching. Each had the physiological swagger of dudes who knew they were enviable to others and regularly traveled well beyond any measured biological constraints. Many had frightening beauty on their arms, women with bewildering bodies and wrist tattoos and modeling contracts who cheered their winners on at races and adored them and gave themselves over to them. There was a vast psychic and economic distance between Julian and them, and they were fast.

He was outclassed before landing in Long Beach. Outclassed on the drive in to Southern California two days prior as a passenger in a car driven by an older racer from his Arizona hometown, a desolate, impoverished blip called Sierra Vista. The moment they hit that run of sprawling cities and bloated houses and giant malls and beautiful mountains and lush foliage and churning industry, which begins at San Bernardino if you're heading west on I-10, they knew they'd entered a kingdom full of promise and hope accessible only to others.

Julian was still wearing shirts that once belonged to his older brother. His bike-racing gear — the jerseys, shorts, bibs, wheels and tires and bikes were professional standard, provided by his team sponsors because he was great at racing road bicycles.

The Pacific Ocean was a few blocks west and visible over barricades, and its cool brackish breeze only reinforced his unease that Southern California was wholly disinviting in its beauty and impossible to roll into and take part of. Nothing about this coastland calmed.

Before heading to the start/finish, Julian stopped at a table in the sign-in area and leafed through a race program. He read several bios of the day's top contenders, which only magnified his lowliness. He was their Dickweed at the OTC:

Al "Deluxe" Box

Team: Strada-Ford Automobiles. Box is two-time U.S. Criterium Champion, placed second at last year's Pan American Games in Men's Team Sprint. The cyclist has countless domestic road and track wins, including the Tour of Redlands, the Grand Prix of Trexlertown, and the California Criterium. Box turned professional this year, is 22 years old and splits his time between Ghent, Belgium and Holmby Hills, California. He is a member of the U.S. National Team.

Barry Howard

Team: Monte/Molteni-Campagnolo

The 23-year-old Howard is a rare breed who can sprint, time trial and climb. He does well on both the road and on the track. He came up on the Junior National Team, took 2nd in the UCI Junior World Championship road race and won the Madison race on the track. Last year he won both the Winston Salem Cycling Classic and The Glencoe Gran Prix and placed second in the Bob Cook Memorial Mount Evans Hill Climb. He spends his downtime perfecting violin skills. Howard hails from Neenah, Wisconsin. He is a member of the U.S. National Team.

Chris Springerville

Team: LeMond-Taco Bell

Ostensibly a track specialist, Manhattan Beach's 25-year-old Springerville is a monster in the final sprint, and has won more than two-dozen top U.S. criteriums in the last two years. He placed second only to Al Box in last year's U.S. Criterium championship. Note that Springerville is the current World Track Champion in the Men's Sprint category and today he'll be wearing the vaunted rainbow jersey, which can only be worn by the one who has proven that he's the best on earth this year.

Julian tossed the program aside, mounted his bike and zigzagged carefully to the start line through noisy throngs of spectators, fans, teams and associates.

The entire peloton was lining up under the roadway-spanning banner that read "Long Beach Grand Prix" in large block letters alongside a dozen corporate-sponsor logos of sports drinks, beer and motor oil.

Jittery with palms wet on brake levers, Julian wheeled slowly through the assembling cyclists and managed a position in the second row, near the podium and beneath the elevated announcer's booth. He'd soon be rubbing shoulders and elbows at high speeds with these men, careening into corners and praying everyone kept their line. He felt tiny and terrified alongside giants.

He kept both feet locked into his pedals and stayed upright by touching the handlebars of an acquaintance named Lon lined up on his right side. Julian figured he'd gain a bike length or two on those around him when the gun sounded because they'd be clipping their shoes to the pedals. He'd be at the front of the group when the pace picked up. Like Freddie said, you don't ever want to be caught at the back of the peloton on a fast, slick course like this one because if the group splits you'll likely never make it to the front and you'll be fighting constantly for the wheel – the slipstream – of the rider in front of you. And if you're caught in the back during a crash, you'll most likely go down too.

Julian knew Lon from the OTC. He was a classic rising Southern California star with golden locks and a hot girlfriend. He even smelled sweet, like wintergreen oil and oranges. Lon looked over at Julian, and shook his head. "Yeah, hold yourself up," he said. "You shouldn't even be in this race. You won't last two laps. Dickweed."

Sometimes you're able to see yourself from outside yourself and Julian could see himself from the elevated vantage of the start/finish podium, his team's colors and sponsorship logos, pink bike and fuckedup complexion. He was just a teenager known to some for his abilities in the mountains, not on closed flat courses that go around and around, these "criteriums," which favor the broad-shouldered sprinters with fast-twitch speed and fearless bike-control skills. Julian's spindly legs resembled weed stems next to the few hundred oiled hypertrophic legs around him.

Julian heard but ignored the distorted mumble of last-minute race instructions from the racecourse referee and reached down and took a swig from his water bottle and returned it to its holder. He trembled and longed to be anywhere else on earth and he needed to puke.

Julian was barely 12 years old when he first shaved his legs, and there was blood all over the bathtub. A trail of blood he'd hoped would lead all the way to the European pro cycling ranks, five thousand miles away. His sisters weren't allowed to shave their legs until they were 15. His parents had no idea Julian shaved his legs, and anyway, they never really knew what their kid was up to most of the time. They knew he rode his bike, but they didn't exactly approve of competitive cycling.

His parents' marriage had gone off the rails before Julian was born. Mom couldn't stand Dad who couldn't stand himself. Dinner table conversations were non-existent, only tired grunts from a dad intolerant to the sound of his children; tense silences interrupted by the sound of slow, reluctant chewing of canned green beans and such Dad-cooked specialties as mushroom soup over thawed waffles from the freezer. Mom rarely made it home after work. She'd occupy any number of mid-town barstools and hotel rooms with her married boss from the downtown office where she worked.

By never congratulating his racing or even acknowledging it — like when he was named to the U.S. National Junior Cycling team — his mom and dad discounted his every living moment. By then he'd traveled to races all over the United States.

Dreams just don't work out, son. You'll wind up flipping burgers.

That way of teaching violence, from father to son, filled the living room with fear, rage and dread. The knuckle-to-bone terror that only a father can administer to his son. But the beatings served a greater, deeper purpose. They were a reward, an offering, a lesson in silent vengeance, and therefore strength, which served to feed Julian's bike-racer fantasies of becoming hard as rock and tough as fuck and fast as the speed of sound.

It meant freedom. The only rules were those dictated by the amount of suffering Julian could tolerate. The suffering cured despair. He'd complete 80-mile solitary training rides on desert and mountain roads before 9:30 a.m. eighth-grade homeroom class.

When word traveled through junior high that the playground-detached Julian shaved his legs and dug punk rock he stomached interminable torment from confounded jocks and cheerleaders and nerds and teachers. It was the same abhorrence reserved for the one lisped kid in school who smelled like piss and made a habit of reaching into his pants and fiddling with his dick.

Fiddler was Julian's only school friend, and they had zero to talk about. But quiet lunches and the smell of piss helped with the isolation and loneliness.

One day an oversized seventh-grader, a Little League baseball hero named Kenny O'Hanion, caught Julian near the tetherball courts on the far edge of the playground. Kenny's dad was a mean alcoholic fireman with forearm tattoos — in an era rare for dads to sport tats unless he served his country or did prison time. Kenny was growing into his dad and in a few years they'd be the same guy. The punches landed hard and fast. The black eyes didn't fade for a week.

The shit-giving continued in high school and Julian's unruly hair and pimples didn't help. He'd endure faces of students, girls and boys, moving toward him in hallways, watch their heads shake and mouths twist into sinister smirks as they approached, and hear contemptible snickers and names like "faggot" and "buttfucker" as they passed. He'd shortcut home through private desert land to avoid schoolyard punches and hassles, but he'd never run or even jog because his legs and body were in endless recovery mode from training – he was either suffering on the bike or recovering from the suffering – and he couldn't upset that delicate physiological balance. *No champion ever would.* But he'd walk fast, and the distance between home and school wasn't too bad, maybe less than a mile.

Julian dropped out of school in tenth grade. His parents had given up on themselves.

Julian had heroes not parents. This was the age of bike-racing innocence, before Lance Armstrong's exceedingly macho and drug-stained American boot stomped so much power and beauty out of the sport. Nine years old back in his bedroom, imitating everything his bike-racing big brother did, and through pictures he cut carefully from old Euro cycling magazines and plastered over his bedroom walls and ceiling, he longed to take on and beat the world's all-time greats.

Julian's heroes were mostly the spindly Spanish cyclists who consistently placed Top 5 in the grand world tours like the La Vuelta España, the Giro d'Italia and the Tour de France. Real-world champs from tiny villages with tomato farmer dads who Julian read about when he was barely strong enough to pedal up a hill.

Big-lunged and power efficient, they were obstinate and reserved, with zero body fat. They earned sulcate sinews and graceful form after having pushed their bodies 100,000 miles. Julian dreamed into their skin and into battles on the Alps and the Pyrenees and the Dolomites. These Spanish crown princes had mad fans throughout Europe, but they suffered for that adoration, some leveraging their bodies far beyond championships and into early graves.

He was 15 when the U.S. Olympic cycling coach informed him he was to be, without question, a true cycling star. Said to just keep his head down and trust him. By that time the kid had already cultivated his darkly competitive attitude and developed scary physical traits. His metabolic efficiency was through the roof, superhuman for a teen. His resting heart rate was 30, and his lung capacity matched older cycling superstars. His young body burned its fat stores first and preserved its limited carbohydrate stores so he could motor faster, harder and longer on races with sustained mountain passes, dropping top racers a decade older and in their physical prime.

It's an addict's need, this yearning and learning to live on risk and pain. Winning teaches you how greatness lurks down deep inside, and quells childhood beat downs that said you don't ever belong anywhere. And that joy of winning — there's something about that kind of joy, it's hard-earned because it rises from a place of pure agony. Hums like the perfect song, the perfect prose, the perfect painting, and your shoes can hold you up above the earth and you're able to walk like that.

Julian was crazy aggressive in his every race, hammering opponents in road races until they shattered. He'd attack and attack and rarely get tired. The victories were visceral, hardly intellectual or even thoughtful. He'd win nearly every contest he entered yet he still didn't know how to win. Freddie recognized that, and was convinced that if he could harvest that raw anger, or whatever it was, develop a rational and circumspect emotional side in the kid, race-strategy acumen and overall wellbeing, he'd have an unstoppable champion. Julian was merely cashing in those father-to-son rewards.

It was Freddie's idea that Julian race this godforsaken nerve fest even though Julian knew he could crash headlong into a wall of concrete at 40 mph and never think right again. He'd guessed that his thinking was already off considering all the suffering he'd so far put himself through on a bicycle.

The pistol shot echoed and Julian leaned hard on his right pedal to gain a bike length on the field in the first 20 feet. He heard a horrible screech and over his shoulder glimpsed Lon sliding sideways, taking six down at least. Lon had a drilled-out crankset and one crank arm broke off when he jumped on it to go. Snapped his ankle in two.

Julian pushed and led the massive peloton around the first hairpin, 300 yards from the start line. The race kicked in at sprint speed and he was ten riders back on the first straightaway. Just like that. Bodies and wheels moved up and up, on all sides, and he hammered in vain to stay near the front of the peloton but was losing positions. To avoid a crash he knew he needed to stay in the top 15. He'd never experienced a race that started this fast, going all out in his biggest gear.

A rider slipped into another and took three down with him. The peloton barreled around the crash.

Julian focused on his own jackhammer breathing and stinging lactic acid collected in his legs when he sprinted for the wheels passing him. His legs felt tired. Why? The day before he took a light, 60-mile ride from his motel near Griffith Park over Topanga Canyon to Simi Valley and back over Santa Susana Pass. Today he was tired, and could barely keep pace, sprinting out of his saddle to stay close to the rear wheels in front of him, in that rider's slipstream. He wished this were a mountain race, but wishing didn't do shit to make him feel better.

A few laps in and Julian counted himself lucky to be upright. Beyond the high-speed shouting and shoving, and there was lots of that going on, it became obvious to all that the race wasn't normal. Newspapers accurately described it later as "a bloodbath." Nearly every hairpin featured a crash that pulled any number of racers down hard. And every crash was similar: there was the sizzle of tires touching, and then skin and nervous systems and state-of-the-art machines cartwheeled and skidded across pavement and into concrete barriers. Top tubes cracked knees and shins, and backbones swiveled in obscene, unnatural directions, and heads bounced along on pavement. The crashes looked and sounded overblown and exaggerated, almost comical in scope, in part due to their frequency, but it was terrifyingly offensive theater.

That rising fear of crashing, the race speed and the slick racecourse itself, all colluded for Julian to quit the race. But Julian could hear his coach's voice repeating. *You can never quit. Never. Even if you know you are to finish dead last, you can't quit. Quitting is addictive. You quit once, you'll quit everything.*

Julian barely hung on to wheels in front of him. He was suffering. *I'm a monster living by the second, he told himself. Bumping elbows and shoulders and wheels and nearly eating shit face-first on asphalt. Endorphins blast my system carrying a life-saving cure to keep "the black dog" off my wheel. I'm hard as rock and tough as fuck and fast as the speed of sound.*

———————

Nobody was quitting this race. First prize purse was five grand. And everybody had a shot. And yet Julian was still losing bike lengths per lap. He went from tenth position to 15th to 20th to 30th to 40th to 50th. After about 40 laps he was near the very back, dodging crashes and sprinting hard to catch back up, alongside frightened mountain race specialists, who were just barely hanging on or were about to either crash or abandon the race. Julian instinctively understood that this is where he belonged, at the back where you must constantly battle yourself and the elements just to hang on, and where you have absolutely no control over your bike if anything should happen in front of you.

Another lap and the sky darkened. The horizon lowered and the rain began. It never rains in Southern California. Julian panicked, rain on an oil-slick course. The first rain-swept corner saw racers falling to Julian's right and left, and his vision blurred in the water and wheels ahead of him spat up wet. Of 100 starters 60 were left. The 40 had crashed or quit. More hairpin turns, more crashes, more blood and skin on the asphalt, but Julian stayed in and on. Somewhere after the 50th lap, just as he was about to pull off and coast to comfort and safety of the start/finish area and the wide frown of his coach, he began to feel better.

He felt the weight of countless mornings hammering on his bike in wee hours while the unattainable girls and beloved baseball boys who hated him were still home in bed, not ready to rise for another three hours to a breakfast made by caring mothers. They'd rise to love and encouragement, to happy dads and air-conditioned rides to school, and an unquestioning hunger for the kind of knowledge offered there.

Julian felt the weight of his father's hand, and it gave him confidence. His heart rate leveled off some so his output wattage wasn't peaking. Strength returned to his legs, and with it more confidence.

He began to feel stronger, bigger, better. Started moving up on people almost effortlessly. For a moment he thought it had something to do with the rain. Or was there a magical ingredient in his water bottle tricking his body, nervous system and muscles?

Al Box, Barry Howard and Chris Springerville were near the front now, as if they appeared from nowhere. The stars had an advantage because each had a teammate alongside them. If you're a race favorite, it's everything to have a teammate, a kind of lieutenant, with you. He protects you, slows the others down if you get away. If you fall back, he'll chase down attacks for you so you can conserve energy. He's your lead-out man in the final sprint.

At two laps to go Julian was nearing the front of the peloton, in the top 15, into the front straightaway. Rain poured down but Julian wasn't sliding on the turns like many others. His bike wasn't slipping out from underneath him. He'd shift as much of his weight on his outside pedal as possible, leaning his body more than he did his bike, keeping the bike more upright when cornering. This way his body stayed relatively balanced over the machine, which compensated for tires losing traction in hidden oil slicks. Julian figured he'd had an additional rain advantage because he weighed less than the big stars who, with their powerful legs and torsos, were built more like speed skaters, all muscle-y and top heavy. The rain slowed the race down too, thereby leveling out Julian's junior-classification gear restriction. He learned he could gain time on turns by not only taking his life into his hands but also because the others were taking fewer risks due to the added slickness.

Julian caught a glance of Box as he moved up, a depressing glimpse of perfect form on the bike, graceful, muscular and sweptback: an up-to-the-moment wisdom of technology and movement, in deep blue and silver team colors. Suddenly the Cali superstar attacked, flew off of the front of the group at a speed that felt double-time, pulling a train of seven riders with him.

Then Howard, who'd been watching Box the entire race, attacked, pulling Springerville and others with him. His effort too was poetic. Julian assessed their demeanor just as he would assess any competitor's demeanor in any other race. He saw no pain in their faces, no fear. All this happened in less than six seconds.

Julian responded. He jump-sprinted around a half-dozen others and caught on to the rear of Howard's five-person train, and his lungs and limbs filled with pain. This group caught Box and company on the back straightaway and Julian recovered quickly. They braked and barely held their lines while negotiating the next hairpin, a few slipped but stayed upright. Out of the turn this 13-man group had a ten-second gap on the peloton, and they were moving, forming an elegant, yet burly, slipstream paceline that saw each rider taking a turn hammering at the front, pulling off and then slipping on to the back of the group while another pulled through and did the same. In this line, Howard stayed glued to Box's wheel.

If this breakaway stayed away to the finish, the race would come down to Box, Howard and Springerville in a sprint to the line.

Racers launched attacks, taking flyers off the front and sides of the group, and Julian could barely keep up the tempo. The peloton behind them picked up speed too.

A crash at the next right-hander nearly pulled Julian down. He was moving too fast into the turn, and then he braked too hard. He leaned into the corner and felt his rear wheel begin to slip. He jerked back into his line at the last possible second, a split second, and saved himself from going down. But he felt a head slam into his rear wheel. It was Springerville. Julian glimpsed back enough to see Springerville's body and head bounce off the freeway and into the barrier and get sucked into watery darkness like a hallucination. Then Julian was out of the saddle and sprinting for life. He hit the straight, put his head down and hammered.

He looked back and saw the breakaway spread barrier to barrier across the freeway section of the course, slowed by Springerville's crash, and he could see the peloton further behind them. Julian plowed, back low and straight, aerodynamic. He stayed inches from the road's concrete barrier, and the crowd and the world on the other side of it, to shield himself from wind and rain spray, and watched the road disappear under his wheels. His legs, these now-perfect pistons, controlled by his heart, and an inner agony that controlled his nervous system, told Julian that his body now had a mind of its own, that no way would it listen to his orders to slow down to keep from hitting the physiological wall. Either his actual mind, or his other mind, he couldn't tell, kept repeating, *I'm hard as rock and tough as fuck and fast as the speed of sound.*

He sucked in and swallowed the city and rainy roadway and pain. He pounded his pedals and felt a million heartbeats. He imagined pierced musclemen with spiked ball-chains in armor behind him, battling for his whiskey, women and gasoline, aboard tricked-out dune buggies and mad chop-shopped school busses armed with hand-crank machine guns, with split skulls and stabbed eyeballs on inside walls, and everywhere rusted rebar and concrete and hot wet sand and misery.

Julian's slim lead evaporated, and by the second hairpin before the front straightaway, the breakaway all but attached itself to his rear wheel. There was a crash as the race snaked around the turn. Julian took a steep line out of the corner and he brushed against the concrete barrier, tearing skin from his elbow. He nearly went down in what would've been a season-ending crash. But instead he attacked, hard. Because he was dangerously close to the barrier heading into the straightaway, on this rain-swept course, no one went with him; to the others, who were all now thinking of the final sprint at the finish line, the 16-year-old zit face Dickweed was but a spindly kid who was lousy in criterium races and had no business being here anyway.

But Julian got away before the final sprint started. He got away before he didn't stand a chance.

He hugged the barrier and hurled through the start/finish area with a five-second gap on the breakaway group. He heard the distorted announcer's voice boom through the racecourse sound system: "One lap to go. One lap to go." And despite crashes and rain, the peloton itself was a serpentine thing of beauty. Its hum silenced the crowd as it passed beneath the start/finish banner 15 seconds behind Julian.

Springerville was out, so that meant that Box and Howard were the two best sprinters in the race. They kept eyes on each other.

The rain fell in sheets and the wind picked up.

I'm a monster living by the second and my head begs me to stop and my blood feels like fire. I'm hard as rock and tough as fuck and fast as the speed of sound.

Julian made time on the next hairpin, nearly going down, and then hammered out the back straightaway, battling a sharp, lifting crosswind. The breakaway group was breathing down the little runaway's neck, a red-tailed hawk on a field mouse. Julian had two seconds on the group by the final hairpin, which he all but slid through.

The internal screaming will not stop. It won't ever stop. Until it does.

Julian looked up from the road and wet and saw the finishing line. He unconsciously jacked fists and arms skyward in victory salute, and a roaring crowd packed thick behind waist-high barriers rushed by on either side, and the announcer's voice barked indecipherables.

Box and Howard, in that order, sprinted across the line two bike-lengths behind Julian, stunned. Behind them, spread across all six lanes, the decimated field of fifty sprinted for fourth place, taken by tree-trunked German sprinter Axel Bohm.

Just beyond the finish line, Box and Howard shot past Julian and angled off toward trainers and girlfriends, arms straight, heads down, waterlogged bodies surrendered. Then the field engulfed the teen from Arizona. Some slapped his back, offered head-shaking congratulations.

Freddie, eyes and arms wide, fat grin, crossed through the racers and jogged toward Julian, armed with towels and water and energy bars, ignoring both Box and Howard, the National Team criterium-sprinter stars. He needed water, he needed a towel, he needed distance from hyper-curious faces crowding him in.

Julian couldn't comprehend what had happened. He'd eluded countless crashes and busted free of that closed circuit of pain and rage.

The next day was a big one in the Southern California mountains, and it went up and down but mostly straightforward.

Spent Saints

Spent Saints

Night lifted off of old Hollywood like an enormous stain slowly evaporating. Spectral visions of dead silent-film stars and spent screenwriters and alcoholic casting agents faded into the humped-back hills. Century City appeared in the dirty distance, a glint of the Pacific Ocean beyond it.

I was laid out in the front room of our sixth-floor apartment. Was it today that my wife was due home from rehab? Next week?

The world was sleepless agony when she'd vanish, sometimes for days on end. Then she'd finally come home, all contrite and contused, purple-yellow streaks and puffed-out needlemarks and little scabby infections on soft skin. The truth is I'd be filled with joy to see her but it was unreasonable because it was really only relief that this woman, the most brilliant and beautiful I'd ever known, who somehow hated herself more than I hated myself, wasn't dead from shooting coke and heroin in the ugliest corners of East Hollywood and downtown L.A. She'd plead forgiveness and make promises and sleep and puke, and we'd fight, but I got to be her savior.

I pushed up and sat at the kitchen table and looked out at the Alto Nido Apartments through the window, a fading Spanish-revival beauty, dark and cold and haunted. Years ago it was a Hollywood beacon, a last stop for film-colony proletariat right as Hollywood curved up into the hills, up into gated walls that housed debauched gin parties and naked flapper girls. I thought of old Joe Gillis, the failed scriptwriter who once lived in the Alto and wound up floating facedown in a mansion swimming pool off Sunset Boulevard. Was Joe fictional? Couldn't recall.

My hands trembled and stank of kerosene. I'd scored crack a few hours earlier off a one-legged black dude. The beer was gone and the liquor stores had closed, which was my worst-ever fear, and I couldn't withstand another coke crash without cushioning.

He stood off the street corner outside of the Alto's entrance, narrow and hazy in a shitty nylon coat. It was cold out, Hollywood wet and luminescent, and I shivered but he wasn't. His one unfilled pant leg flapped in the breeze and he smelled of scorched sulfur and despair. A few more slips and I'll be right here next to him. I said, "Meth or powder?"

He shook his head and looked away. I might as well have been some desperate asshole agent from Sherman Oaks manning his shiny Audi into shit Hollywood in the wee hours looking to *score some blow, man.*

I waited for his shrug and followed him around a corner and behind a Dumpster. His air of condescension was no different from countless agent, record company, and film studio people I'd met in L.A. He hobbled on that bowed crutch with its rotted underarm pad and handgrip and produced a baggy that had a dozen or so jagged rocks in it.

He raised a glass pipe, dropped in a taste, placed his cracked lips around the open end, fired it up and huffed. The lighter flashed up a glistening, creviced face, a lazy-lidded eye and a diamond stud in each ear, and he managed well with quivering hands. He pulled the pipe from his mouth, squeezed his eyes shut, tilted his head back and exhaled. Riches.

He hoisted the pipe toward my face, loaded and lit it. I sucked. Held it in. The heart kicked open and blood vessels ballooned. Coughed like a motherfucker and Hollywood went sideways and a choir of punk rock angels slammed my ears.

I pulled all I had from my front pocket — two crumpled tens — and handed them over. He dropped two rocks into my palm and I turned and left. After a half block I stopped and looked back. Saw a Hollywood dream merchant, a silhouette propped up on a bent crutch in a triangle of streetlight. I hurried the few blocks home down Franklin Avenue.

I had no pipe because I didn't smoke crack. Not ever. So I crushed the little rocks and stuck bits into the head of a Marlboro from a pack my wife stashed in a kitchen drawer. She'd smoke them when we'd climb out through the window onto the fire escape at night to take in the strange beauty of Los Angeles.

The Marlboro crack eased the coke crash and a skittish sort of relief settled over me. I drifted through the fake French doors that opened to the skyline above Highland Avenue and then up and over Mulholland Drive. Saw a dozen shades in the sky in a cold Los Angeles morning, saw dim stars refract off hillside swimming pools and perfect rows of palm trees stretching skyward as if to glimpse the ocean. Even the palm trees wanted a better life.

The relief was short-lived. Soon the full weight of my head dropped into my hands and sickening dread rose in direct proportion to the misery of the rising sun. Then the night came back.

The Spent Saints had gigged earlier at a packed Bar Deluxe, a shithole on Las Palmas just above Hollywood Blvd, which held, maybe, 200 people. A good crowd showed to see us, including a couple of VP's from different major record labels. Lick Stubinski arrived not long before we went on. He made his entrance with an entourage. The crowd cleared a path for him as he moved through it. It was like he was floating.

Lick is a famous record producer, in the old-school way. Like Phil Spector he got famous for making records that became famous. He made his name creating brilliant albums that made careers of deserving artists who had something real to say and the passion and ability to say it. It made his own star rise until he was as big as the stars he'd produced, if not bigger. But along the way Lick's work became about money not art. He's The Starmaker now, and with his flowing robes, pointy beard and affected introspective energy, he moves like some stoner maharaja.

A trusted pal who'd spent months recording with Lick said he's still just a pothead with a predilection for blow and video games, whose massive anal porn collection fills an entire room in his house. There's your transcendence. I'd heard Lick dug our band.

The record company folk were equally clownish. At least the ones I'd met, especially those older than 35 and still strolling around wearing Converse. It may be oversimplification but all I saw were guys making bank off songwriters, as if they'd actually written the songs themselves. I saw who counted the money first. I knew music's heyday was long gone.

Clusters of white scenesters with perfect skin blocked

bar lanes and bathrooms. I slid onto a bench in the dressing room and lubed up on Foster's Lager. Even after a thousand shows I needed to get crocked to perform. Crocked I had some confidence and crocked was the only way I could get in front of people. Booze turned onlookers into faceless smears on the periphery, made expressions unreadable. The breathless melody, energy, rhythm and sexual tension in the music become the universe and you're its center. In your mind that's huge responsibility and one slip into a self-conscious moment, like, say, realizing your zipper's been down for an entire song, and it's all over. It's narcissistic as hell too because amped-up self-hatred produces the kind of attention whoring that can't be duplicated in daily life, or, really, in any other profession. The biggest self-centered pieces of shit are always found in the arts, especially in the performance kind. But all of that wanes when everything is on, and in that extraordinary instance, fronting a great rock & roll band is better than anything. Makes living the day-to-day pretty damn hard.

As a band we were either great or god-awful. You're not worth a drop of beer in the hell of your own failing ambition when you're awful. Most often it's like that, an idiot train of miscues and overly enthusiastic drinking and self-mockery, and you long for an enormous hook to appear from stage left to yank you from your misery, which means there's never a reason to show your face in a venue afterward. When Spent Saints were great it was wingless flight. That's the drug you chase.

And none of us were great musicians, but we played off each other, sometimes grasped for dear musical life off each other. And we internalized each other's obsessions and turmoils, and so the music came out fully formed. That's what made us a band. That's what makes any band a band.

Against a backdrop of power chords and three-minute shout-alongs, I strutted, leapt, shouted and shook the hips, a purely subconscious dictation of movement inspired equally by the wallop behind me and boyhood idols Jagger, Alice and Rotten, in service to a personal god who's a trashy mix of some carnival barker on speed and Nike of Samothrace. My four bandmates participated fully in the rock-show pageantry, ducked and side-kicked out of my way, and a kohl-eyed sea of raven-headed bodies crammed to the front of the stage.

We finished in an ear-ringing, two-encore mess of aching wet limbs, rumpled fringes and split creepers. It was a rare show because it felt right, intemperate and unrestrained. I exited the stage on a cloud of endorphins and went straight for the beer because, of course, there's nothing like feeling great to make you want to feel greater. As I neared the dressing room, strangers swarmed, faces beamed, and palms slapped my back; new fans who'd purchased CDs from our merch table wanted me to sign them. This center-of-the-universe thing wasn't me; I wanted the attention but when it came I couldn't do it.

Fortunately I was hammered, and happy. For a fleeting moment I felt deserving. But flattery only sets you up for despair and for me more reason to anesthetize myself.

Two drop-dead women were looking at me while talking to each other, as if I were subject of their conversation. Noticed them earlier because no one can ignore perfected Southern California bloodlines. They're superhuman. The dusty blond wore hip-huggers and boots and had arched brows and sullied innocence like Marianne Faithful in 1967, and the other, with ombre hair and winged eyeliner, was wholly unapproachable. They filled my head and heart with longing. Angels. In my eyes they each offered rectitude, a salvation, and some kind of

enlightenment. Then reality descended and I remir
that I was at best a scaled-down repro of a person w
women really want — I'm not confident or fearless (
earner or some androgynous smartass or half interesting. I was
afraid to talk to either of them. And I had a wife in rehab.

Some eager band readied the stage to perform and the club
emptied. My guys and a couple of tubby roadies, Mac and
Cheese, loaded the gear into the van and headed off to our Eagle
Rock rehearsal space to unload. I was about to hit Mac and
Cheese up for a lift home, but decided to hoof it. I dug walking
Hollywood midnights because it's strangely peaceful if you're
off the boulevards. You don't get hassled like you do in daylight.
I was more at home around trannies and drunks and street
urchins and ghosts and corner dealers than club kids and rock-
show attendees, most of whom never drank well, owned alarm-
beeping cars and lived buffered lives on family money streams.
I preferred brown, beat-up neighborhoods.

As I was about to leave, a nose-high thin guy wearing Buddy
Holly specs approached and pulled me aside. No handshake, no
introduction. He wore a high-collar pink shirt and slim-cut suit,
with close-cropped, bleach-blonde hair. Moved with that West
L.A. affect, an air of self-importance and push-tit confidence.
Was there a bar somewhere in this city where people go and get
drunk on self-belief, on impudence? If so, that's where I wanted
to be, nightly. I liked his suit.

"Lick Stubinski saw your show," he said.

"Yeah, I saw him," I said. "Pretty fucking cool. Who are
you?"

"Dante, Lick's assistant."

A famous person's assistant is famous too, especially one
called Dante. Their indifference toward you is obvious. They

walk around as if they have knowledge of something important that you don't.

I said, "Yeah, I saw Lick. He kinda floats in and hovers, huh?"

Dante didn't respond. His eyes shifted to Lila, Towner's lovely girlfriend. Towner is one of two Spent Saints' guitarists. Lila and Towner were joined at the hip.

I motioned to Lila, said, "Dude. Her boyfriend's right behind you."

Dante looked at me blankly and pushed a show flyer into my hand with an address scrawled on the back, a place in the hills. "Lick would like it if you and that skinny guitarist would come up to his house tonight. He can bring his girlfriend. Don't invite anyone and don't ever give anyone that address."

I wadded the flyer into my pocket, snapped open a fresh oilcan of beer and drained a good third in one swig. I said, "OK, dude. My name's Julian Grayling, by the way."

Dante nodded once with eyebrows raised and turned and walked away.

Fifteen minutes later, me, Towner and Lila were in her Honda rolling toward Beverly Hills. I had the whole backseat and Lila had the wheel. Towner and me worked our beers.

It irritated us that Lila kept her radio tuned to KROQ, but the station played one of a few great songs from the 1980s, a concoction of sad drone and lilting power pop called "Heaven." It pumped the rear woofers and Southern California rushed through open windows into my face and created one of those burning melancholies that resonate deep inside. Its melody intensified and the alcohol and endorphins worked their magic against the night. I took in sweet orange and jasmine blossoms. The muted streetlight halos lifted unevenly up the hills on winding roads into the black, into my imagined heaven of the dead, until Dennis Wilson and Ramon Novarro and old Buk and creepy Manson girls and *Rock 'n' Roll High School* and Laurel Canyon crammed all corners of my skull. The Honda rolled smoothly up the Hollywood Freeway, heading northwest over Cahuenga Pass, and the hills behind us closed down the jeweled lights of old Hollywood.

We soon eased off the 101 onto Ventura Blvd and turned south up Beverly Glen. We crossed Mulholland, the back way into Benedict Canyon where Lick's house was located.

What I'd heard about Lick Stubinski is he never got angry, ever. Not at anyone. Not at his cook, not at a singer who couldn't hack it in the studio, and not at girlfriends, assistants, leeches, and so on. Stayed calm at all times. Was, as they say in L.A., "deep as shit."

By 1 a.m. I was sitting beside Towner and Lila sucking pharmaceutical grade lines off a low-rising wrought-iron table of thick beveled glass, our asses planted on big tasseled floor pillows. The table could seat maybe a dozen people and had a sizable vase holding as many fresh purple orchids. The room opened to an outdoor poolside pavilion and garden and 180-degree views of L.A.

Lick's sprawling crib was whitewashed and wood beamed and Asian rugged, as if plucked from Spain's Mediterranean coast in some other century and placed atop a snaking road in Beverly Hills. Everything built into the house had a story written long before Lick was born, the elaborate butterfly mosaics patterned into vast imported floors, the frescos, and the built-in floor-to-ceiling mahogany bookshelves, which Lick had filled with vintage tomes dealing in metaphysics, and Hindi linguistics, and Buddhism. He was just a tourist here.

The house allowed you to look down on a world of privilege

splayed out at your feet, a house where only stars go higher. It had to rub off. We'll never know Lick's kind of wealth but I guessed it easily transcended any misery his own guilt could ever whip up.

Two assistants — Dante and some other dude— moved mechanically in and out of the room as if adhering to instructions from Lick only they could hear. A handful of women, all prepossessing in a kind of hill-country porno way, drifted in the periphery and out on the terrace. Heard someone say they danced at Crazy Girls. I recognized one from porn, a Dumb Angel contract girl who recently got popped because she handed parental duties of her two toddlers over to the female head of a porn production company — no need for complicated adoption papers or intrusive screenings to safeguard against shitty parenting. Her children got in the way of how famous she thought she was going to be. The state discovered the dirty adoption and fostered the kids out.

Spotted a pair of bloated, '80s hair-metal stars with unfortunate receding hairlines, no doubt hoping that if they loitered long enough, Lick would magically restore their careers to stadium status. A squirrely white rapper with unsettling energy and bobbing head bounced around the room.

Towner recognized him. "That's that rapper from Detroit."

"Chainsaw?" I said. "Funny. Doesn't look like Detroit."

"Says he is."

"Whatever," I said. "You know Chainsaw's shtick is marketing spin for street cred. You can tell he's no Detroiter for real. His energy's suburban — he's too loud and self-entitled, too soft and white."

"It's no wonder he's about to break huge in America," Towner said.

Chainsaw began talking at a couple of girls and his rehearsed city slang sounded nasally like a stammering cockatoo, and his arms waved around. A pair of burly black bodyguards stood tall behind him, wrists crossed at their waists. They dripped of menace, like Detroit.

I said, "It's always the white guys ripping off black music who get huge."

Towner nodded.

"R&B, soul, rock & roll, reggae, rap," I said. "It's our history."

"Pretty much," Towner said. "Look at Arthur Alexander. Covered by fourteen of the best white fuckers ever — The Beatles, Stones, Elvis, Dylan and the Bee Gees, and he wound up driving a bus."

"Makes us pretty fucking insignificant?"

Towner shrugged and hit his beer.

Lick made his entrance. He was barefoot in a gut-accenting crimson dhoti different from the one he sported at the venue. He carried a spliff, a velvet pouch and a bottle of something expensive. He placed the bottle on the table — aged cognac — and pulled from the purse a large baggie filled with coke and dumped it out on the dwindling pile in front of us. He prepared another heap on the table's far side for the others. There wasn't a soul in the house who missed that maneuver. He plopped down beside me cross-legged on a pillow, opened the cognac, poured into two glasses on the table, lighted and hit the massive blunt, turned to me, extended the weed, exhaled, winked and said, "Hey Spent Saint, help yourself."

I said, "Dude, thanks. But got any beer?"

Lick motioned Dante over, ordered beer and dismissed him with a patronizing Sufi sleight-of-hand.

"Whatever you want," Lick said, "he'll get for you."

I watched Dante trot to the kitchen and felt sorry for him.

He returned with a bucket of iced Heinekens and an opener and placed them between Towner and me. Towner dug in and served us.

Lick pointed out two girls in the room, said, "Those chicks? Don't talk to them." The way he called them his "chicks" sounded like he'd made them into handy caricatures — comely walkons to serve the ever-erudite and intellectualizing producer. Then he crouched over the table, vacuumed a rail into his right nostril, closed his eyes and leaned his head back. He bounced his forefinger off the glass, said with watery eyes and a throaty exhale, "This table belonged to John Gilbert. Dude got 20,000 fan letters a week — until the talkies came in. They said his voice was too funny-sounding for stardom."

"Like mine," I said.

Lick sat back, continued: "His career was over. Just like that."

The beard gave Lick an Appalachian face and his lips looked like bubblegum stuck to the ass of a sheep dog, pink and puffy and strangely feminine. His perfectly white (save for one or two capped gold) teeth gnashed together between sentences, sometimes on sentences. Hoped my jaws didn't look like that. You never could tell with coke this good. He thumbed over his shoulder, added, "Gilbert's place was a couple blocks away from here."

I went down for another line. No burn. Pure. Great shit. Sparklehorse sounded godlike on the stereo.

Blow is in my experience a drug carried by douchebags who dole it out to you because they think you're worth a shit. You're not. And they're not. It's a circle jerk.

"He drank himself to death before he was 40," I said. "Gilbert. At one point he had it all."

Lick nodded. "That's right. Set for life. He probably had a harem and all the opium, cocaine, cash and top-shelf booze you could ever wish for. The decadence."

"Not such a bad way to go," I said.

I thought of old John Gilbert, matinee star. Dumped by the movie studio, dumped by Greta Garbo, dumped by millions of fans. Hammered, heartbroken, alone up in these hills. No wonder he fell over dead at 38.

Heavy arched doors with gate-latch handles had opened to the veranda and I swore I felt ghosts of fearless Hollywood drunks out there rustling in the brush and trees and hanging around homes that haven't yet been torn down and replaced by cheese-whiz clapboard mansions cut into hillsides that teen stars pay $20 mil for. Legendary alchy Alice Cooper once had a place near here too, up where film star John Barrymore drank himself to death decades earlier. Somehow Cooper had survived culture shifts, had come back, unlike Gilbert. Valentino lived up around the bend.

"Nobody knows who the fuck Gilbert was," Lick added. "You're the only person I've ever met who does."

"This town was heroic once," I said.

"Fuck, still is," Lick said. "It's fucking amazing. You just need to know how to win."

I hated people who talked of life and existence in terms of winning and losing, especially one who when sober espouses in interviews to be an interpreter, and fervent practitioner of eastern philosophies and peaceful existences.

Lick had one of those stereos that costs as much as a house.

His listening choices, conversely, steeply contradicted the sound and feel of his more recent production choices: Before Sparklehorse we heard some James Carr and Townes Van Zandt, all pumped through two enormous tube amplifiers and six-foot speakers so thin they resembled freestanding minimalist wall art.

"Listen," Lick said, "we need to talk about the Spent Saints songs."

"Yeah?" I said. "Really?"

Towner and Lila had stepped out to the veranda to smoke cigarettes. They looked good together, like a real couple. Lila had been for a few years indulging Towner's inner rock & roll, but she was really into getting a house and having a baby, and then maybe another, with Towner. I understood what she saw in him. He was sweetness personified, and beautiful, like, as Lila once pointed out to me, Donatello's second statue of David; he was all hope and dreams not yet wasted on a festering alcohol addiction. Poor Lila couldn't even imagine the pain heading her way.

"Look, man, just because a song is done does not mean it's finished," Lick said. "And what's with all this feminine shit? You guys are a fucking rock & roll band." His brow furrowed, and he said, "There will be no faggy fake poets in my studio."

Lick could talk. His verbiage trampled over the best songs that played. He showed zero responsiveness each time some stunner flowed from the speakers. I don't trust people who don't hear that stuff, who miss those moments that summon that place inside of you where sadness and wonder cut to the very heart of your existence; those rare songs that paralyze you in your tracks no matter where you are when you hear them.

Neil Young's "Out on the Weekend" came on and that

sourceless ache stirred inside. Lick yakked and I watched his jaws work and that knotted hemp necklace bounce along in time just under his Adam's apple, and I knew in that moment that nothing could ever come from Lick's mouth, or anyone's mouth, that could better the chorus of "Out on the Weekend."

But Lick yammered on. "… We need to get the balls in there, man. …"

When I think of, say, "Out on the Weekend," "balls" is the furthest thing from my mind. When the song ended I asked Lick straight up if he really wanted to "produce" us?

"Why else would you be sitting in my house if I wasn't planning on producing you?"

His eyes were too close together and then too close to mine. I examined the dark gray speckles that floated around his cocaine-expanded pupils. And his hair was fading Biblical, all middle-aged thin and graying above the temples and forehead. I knew that if this guy produced us we'd be on our way as a band.

I saw Lila and Towner outside on the veranda. Towner was pointing out stars for her.

"Get ready," Lick said. "You guys are going to be huge."

Lick got up and excused himself to piss as Curtis Mayfield's "Wild and Free" came on. Something swelled inside again and I had this image of the Spent Saints on a trajectory of fame, the kind that could cancel hopelessness, the kind that sanctified childhood dreams of rock & roll stardom and could elevate the soul to some transcendent plane. I felt untouchable. The world around me was in servitude to the song, to my elation. Then came the Stones' "Moonlight Mile," an emotional suckerpunch that could stir even the ghosts of these hills.

Lick returned, snorted a massive line and yakked right over "Moonlight Mile." "I'm tellin' you, man — you guys have it all, the sexuality, the songs, the hooks, the commitment." His slight Jersey honk, which couldn't be smoothed out even with obvious speech coaching, got worse the more coke he snorted. "Some melodies sound too sissy. We can easily correct that. And toughen you up, and …"

I cut in. "It's all feel, man. That's all that is. Gives me the goosebumps. It sounds corny as shit but we need to find some grace in the center of things. Otherwise, what's the point?"

"You need *balls*," he said.

Even coked out, attempting to explain songs to a producer hailed as genius for once creating brilliance but who lately had been producing what I considered to be some of the shittiest rock and rap on earth was like, as Billy Bragg famously said a long time ago, talking poetry to the taxman.

I realized that music for Lick is the antithesis of artisanal; it's mechanical, an assembled means to an end, service music with a fat paycheck attached. Fist-pumping refrains for boys, and the young girls with them who haven't yet found a place in the world. A new Lick-produced song was a moment squashed into a box and played back while the listener's doing something else that requires real attention. Lick's a producer but he no longer *got* music.

I looked around at the books, and the house, and the people and realized it was all show – props in Lick's lavish universe of pseudo-transcendence. It was spiritual Auto-Tune. I realized too that if Lick produced Spent Saints we'd lose whatever integrity we had. I was once a major fan of his productions, how he could distill a song to its essential essence while exposing the artist's greatness. I wanted that Lick, the one from a decade prior.

Lila and Towner returned to their pillows and we all huffed up more lines. The coke felt great and our hearts raced and the horseshit really began to burp out. When talk switched from organic gardening to pop-up religions, Lila, whose manner and expression turned more serious, and almost vicious-eyed, the higher she got, as if every word she uttered carried weight, said, "Look, we're all a bunch of self-entitled assholes, right? Our histories are in dark arts and pandemic made-up religions, right? ..."

I had to cringe but I hated to. Lila's hands under the table were opening and closing quickly, involuntarily, and her knees were bouncing a mile a minute. No matter how high you get, or what kind of a coked-out asshole you are, it's never fun to watch a bright and beautiful woman make a cocaine ass of herself.

"... Right, right, right," Towner chimed in. "And a thousand years ago Charlie Manson would've had his own religion and empire with a huge harem, just another insane warlord king running Europe, challenging European slaves to rise to challenge the Muslims and to free their slaves. ..."

I was a cocaine asshole now. Every facet of existence lived and breathed: books, chairs, tapestries, rugs, candles, songs, faces, windows, art, Lila, Towner, Lick, strippers, Chainsaw, all of it.

Shit was closing in.

Lick interrupted, "Roman Polanski and Sharon Tate's house was just around the corner where Manson's gang slaughtered Tate and man-hair star Jay Sebring and others back in the summer of '69. You think that was an accident? Manson had the gift to sway the chicks. You gotta give him that. He could've been a rock star in those days. People tried to help him get a record deal. Some rock stars still will never admit to helping him out. They saw how Manson had the rock & roll formula down: you get the chicks and the dudes show up for the action.

One member of, I think, the Beach Boys — Brian Wilson — tried hard to help him, recorded one his songs, and the Manson clan sponged off him at his house …"

I butted in. "Nope, It was Dennis Wilson."

"Right," he said. "Whatever."

"How could you of all people get that one wrong?" I said.

I shook my head, looked away. I saw this house, and the rest of Beverly Hills, catch fire and slide down the hill and melt into the Pacific Ocean.

I focused on a woman across the room. She sat on a red velvet throne-type chair in front of the picture window. Bone thin in fuck-me heels. Every 15 minutes or so she'd step over for a line, her thinning blond locks thickened with poorly hidden weaves falling over the top of her head onto the pile of coke. Stainless-steel coke snorter gripped by bony fingers, heliotrope veins snaking up the back of her hands. She closed her left nostril with her left forefinger and vacuumed a line into her right nostril, and then quickly switched nostrils and did the same. Then she flipped her head and hair back, squeezed her nostrils shut with two fingers and held that pose for too long. No one noticed her. I did. She had chemically enhanced lips and cheekbones, lifted eyes, wildly age-inappropriate hip-huggers and a wrist tattoo of barbed wire with dangling hearts. She wore a black sheer top under a too-new biker jacket, her silicon tits sat high and shelved. She paid too much attention to her body too late in life. I felt for her.

Then I recognized her. Sure, it was what's-her-name, TV star from the '80s. I elbowed Towner, nodded at the woman. "Dude, is that what's-her-name … ?"

Towner was fast with useless pop shit. He looked at me, her.

"Jesus, that is," Towner said. "That's Bebe Hailey, *Playboy*

Playmate, huge TV star in the late '70s, '80s. God. What happened to her?"

At some point Bebe Hailey became a mockery of herself, a bit player in the obscene Hollywood narrative of obsolescence. Reclined on that antiquated sitter, framed by Beverly Hills in the window, she was lost, broken. I fought off images of our own future lives, the disconnections, sadnesses, and agonies. This is where it all leads.

Lick continued to go off about the Beach Boys. His words tightened my stomach. Then it busted out. I said, "You're a fuckin' producer and you dismiss the Beach Boys? Don't even know Dennis from Brian? That makes you an asshole on two counts: One, you're a self-aggrandizing shill for the record companies, and this whole fucking town, and, two, you don't know the band that defined California culture, from the beaches to the hills to the underbelly of the Manson era to your very own transcendental meditation … Unfuckingbelievable …"

Towner and Lila dropped jaws. Towner leaned in. "Julian, fuckin' chill."

I paused and looked out at the city far below. "Fuck this pompous dipshit."

Lick's voice rose. "Because I hate the fuckin' Beach Boys?"

I turned to Lick. "Pretty much."

He erupted. "Who the fuck are *you*? You should be grateful to be in my house, drinking my alcohol. You are here for my amusement, not the other way around, asshole. Whatever flaws you see in me are only a projection of you; you're showing yourself who you are. You need to accept that and put your ego away. …" Lick actually said that. Towner and I looked at each other at precisely the same moment. Best friends.

Others turned to the action. I zeroed in on the coke suet and sweat on Lick's neck and forehead. It looked like the substance on faces of table bussers at truckstop diners.

"Fuck *you*, and fuck the Beach Boys," Lick shouted.

Right then a select 4 a.m. crew arrived. Doll parts in designer labels on arms of millionaire fake punk rockers, another famous rapper and entourage. Lick left the table in disgust and stammered out onto the deck, down beyond the long swimming pool. His pair of girls followed him out.

Towner pressed into me, insisted we split. He was right. I knew I'd just blown any chance the Spent Saints had with superstar-maker Lick.

Anyway, Lila had work in a few hours. I hurriedly scooped coke from the pile into the show flyer that had Lick's address on it and folded it into my pocket. As long as I had some reserve I'd be OK. Grabbed the last Heineken and we got out of there. Could feel Dante closing in.

We got to the car. The engine kicked over. Wheels spun, and I pressed my hand over the pocket that contained the drugs to protect it.

We zoomed along Mulholland and I ignored the stars and the sweet night blossoms. Towner leaned over the seat, said, "Well, Julian, that's that." We powered up the windows and I broke out the stolen blow. We laughed and talked and shouted our asses off as we rolled down out of the hills snorting up that shit. By the time we pulled in front of my building in Hollywood, the blow was about gone. We snorted the last of it idling in front of my building. No way Lila was getting any sleep before her work shift started. Here come crashes.

The squall would stop and then it would start in again.

Screeeeee, dweedle-dweedle-dee-dee, dweedle-dweedle-dee-dee, dweedle-dweedle-dee-deeeeeee … like trucks running over kittens. *Screeeeee, dweedle-dweedle-dee-dee, dweedle-dweedle-dee-dee, dweedle-dweedle-dee-deeeeeee, Screeee* … coming from next door. It pierced the apartment's thick, 80-year-old walls.

My Asian neighbor kid, a guitarist full of amped-up, out-of-time energy: *Dweedle-dweedle-dee-dee-dweedle-dweedle-dee-dee* … The kid was torturing a tune from Lick's catalog of shitty hip hop-metal productions.

Knuckles rapped the front door. *Screeeeee dweedle-dweedle-dee-dee-dweedle-dweedle-dee-dee* … I looked out at old Hollywood, the sun burning through its two-toned scuzz. People strode sidewalks with a purpose I didn't understand. Harleys with cocked-up pipes spluttered down Wilcox Avenue toward the boulevard, and a car motor turned over repeatedly but wouldn't start. I squinted the Alto Nido into view. Smelled cat piss and kerosene. I could barely lift my arms.

It started again. *Screeeeee, dweedle-dweedle-dee-dee-dweedle-dweedle-dee-dee, dweedle-dweedle-dee-de- dweedle-dweedle-dee-dee* … *Screeeeee* … It stopped.

Heard bags flop on the hallway floor, some rustling. The doorknob turned, stopped. Locked. The low rumble of a man's voice and a woman's.

Heard the clatter of keys and one entering the lock. Felt the air pressure change in the apartment when the door swung open. My wife was home from rehab, with, I think, her dad.

Eye for Sin

Eye for Sin

I climbed into the passenger seat and Tinkles lifted the pint of Southern Comfort from between his legs and offered me a shot. Took a good chug, handed it back and twisted an air conditioning vent in my direction. Pretty much all we needed to say to each other.

Tinkles wheeled the old Corolla back out onto my street, and turned west on Van Buren. We took it easy through downtown, headed north on Seventh Ave. and rolled toward Sunnyslope, a dark burb that rises up a sun-crested hill. There were few cars out and butter-colored streetlights fanned across the windshield. Tinkles flipped the car stereo on to Cher's "Believe," and turned it up. I reached out and turned it down. Blown distorted speaker, horrible song. Ears didn't want it.

"Jesus gonna be there?"

Tinkles nodded and flicked the volume back up.

It was near midnight and Tinkles arrived two hours late. See, waiting to score crystal was madness. All you do is fret and pace. You count minutes and seconds. You count the books on your shelves and the stars in the sky and the zits on your face and how many craps you took that week. You count everything, again and again. And the very first tweeker pathology you learn is that they are *never* on time. But you wait. You count. Every time. Fucking madness.

Before we got to Sunnyslope we swung by a Circle K and picked up a forty of King Cobra for me and a couple of quarts of Bud for Tinkles and Jesus. I never showed up without a bottle for the host.

I'd met Jesus once. It was nighttime and he was leaning against a tree. He talked at me for two hours in that way that people do when they're used to being the only one talking. It was more of a sermon involving his missing son and Phoenix's white-pride underground and the New Testament's immortal worms of hell and the agony of doing crystal meth in prison because it puts you in another prison and you end up beatin' your limp dick in the shower stalls for 24-hours straight.

Neighborhood folks said Jesus was a good Christian, christened him "Jesus of Sunnyslope." He was a New Testament fanboy who strode the hood at night armed with a bible and holstered sidearm, and he treated the streets and those on them as his ministry. They said he had a big heart. They said he protected them. He helped moms with coins for the Laundromat and gave money to those whose food stamps were spent. They said he'd never sell to minors. To score meth off him you had to prove you were older than 18. They said he decapitated some dude once with a guitar string for raping a Sunnyslope girl. A dealer with a heart of gold.

I'd figured prison taught him rules, like how to live by fear, and to rule by it. He controlled the crystal flowing in and out of Sunnyslope. That gave him emotional control. He was the neighborhood protector so the residents owed him. He threatened real violence with guns and a quick-burn fuse. He had eyes and muscle in dark corners of the hood.

We were meeting him because the west side hillbillies were dry. He was never in short supply of good shit, but it had a price: you had to endure him. We needed crank and me and Tinkles laughed that the route to god was through Jesus. Any other time I'd hate his guts.

Skeletal trees, chain-linked dirt yards and cinderblock-box houses constructed so close together on narrow streets made the hood feel claustrophobic. More than one open door revealed a motorcycle parked in a living room and too-loud big-screen TVs. I saw sallow faces in joyless interiors lit up in reality show colors, the hues of celebrity deification and yearnings for easy fame and wealth. It gave the illusion of living in vibrant lights. Hi-def desperation fueled on meth, fantasy. Police cruiser lights brightened up the all-hour action, cops in real time. Crystal kept the entire neighborhood wired.

The street grew darker the nearer we got to Jesus's place. It looked pieced together from black-and-white photos of decades-old crime scenes. His was last on the left on a hilltop dead-end, and beyond that a no-man's land of sharply barbed cacti and jagged rocks descending into darkness.

"Dude, *Heart of Darkness*," I said.

Tinkles didn't respond. He rarely did. He was a reserved dude with a lisp. A comment from him felt like an intrusion. But he was no idiot. He'd bailed from journalism school. In the years I'd known him I'd never heard more than a single sentence, maybe two, drop from his mouth at any one time. He once drunkenly confided that his lisp provided endless hours of agony, especially around girls.

Tinkles flipped a bitch and parked in front of Jesus' place. He killed the motor and headlights, and swallowed the last of his pint. Streetlights were shot out but we had moonlight. I stepped out of the car and into the hot breeze. Unscrewed the King, swallowed a good one and took in Phoenix splayed out in the valley below. Darkness always calms the city's harsh edges, and the glimmering reds and ambers comforted. The malt liquor was ice-cold and I was feeling better.

Jesus's house was hidden behind shit piled high in the fenced front yard. A burnt husk of a Ford Bronco was centerpiece and heaped around it were bedsprings, busted motorcycle frames, a corroded washing machine, a doorless refrigerator, a man-tall plastic Santa, mangled swing-set, and all sorts of junk. Weeds grew up through the chaos and you could taste the rust on your tongue. A barricade passing itself off as some blue-collar art installation depicting a meth-damaged vision of Eden.

Tinkles stepped from the car and a raging pit bull emerged from under the junk and scared the shit out of us. We sprinted up Jesus's dirt driveway and I followed Tinkles around the house to a side entrance. Now Tinkles is the only overweight tweeker I'd ever met, maybe the only one who'd ever existed, so his trot had me howling. I'd never seen him attempt to run. He looked like one of those old Weebles toys, wobbling side-to-side, but with globs of jiggly flesh threatening to split his maroon work slacks and pop buttons from his shirt. Even he laughed.

The side entrance was half hidden by dead vines. We ducked to avoid a smashed up security camera dangling from a cable off its mount.

We knocked. Waited. Knocked again. Waited. Tinkles unpinned his work-shirt nametag and slid it into his pant pocket. We knocked again, longer this time. Panic rose. Every cell in my body screamed for meth. I unscrewed the King and sucked. God bless the King of Malt Liquor. The peephole darkened. Another moment passed. We heard voices on the other side of the door. Another moment passed. Christ! Then multiple deadbolts clicked and, finally, the door swung open.

We stepped inside and tweeker effluvia filled our faces and I almost choked on what smelled of underarms and peeled onions and lawn mowers.

A woman stepped from behind the door and acknowledged us. She was skinny, skull-eyed, dirty blond and pregnant, a pole in faded pastels with a hump in the middle and two heartbeats, one of which was visible in her neck, speed-thumping away. She shut the door behind us and vanished like a ghost down the dark hallway. She had no presence, emanated nothing, and left little impression. People ravaged by crystal meth are like that; like something tangible in their being — astral planers say "aura" — had been eaten away. You see them physically but they're lighter in every sense of the word.

A Confederate flag stretched across the ceiling, nailed up in the center and corners, backlit by the ceiling bulb. Gave off a blood-red tint of hate.

You couldn't miss Jesus. He was centered on the bed in the corner, shirtless against the wall with a lipped smoke. He had concave eyes with Manson's leer and waxy Willie Nelson hair.

He was carving up a fist-sized hunk of wood in quick smooth gestures. Shavings collected on his forest of chest hairs and wrinkly swastika between his nipples. He didn't look up at us.

He pulled a forearm over his sweaty brow and examined his handiwork, the beginnings of a half-lidded human eye. "I'll put it to practical use," he said, and resumed whittling.

A dozen dead eyes looked down on us from perches on the wall— mule deer, pronghorn antelope, javelina. Lighted maps of Arizona and Montana ate up wall space and each sported a number of little red flags pinned strategically between Podunk towns nowhere near interstates. The flags represented operations run by militias and Holocaust deniers that Jesus pontificated about the night I'd met him. Hierarchies of fear based on prison-yard pecking orders, where empathy and insight were taboo.

"Scottie," Jesus said. "How's my man?"

Tinkles grinned, waved quickly, and said, "Hey, Jesus."

"This the writer you was tellin' me about?" Jesus still hadn't looked up.

Tinkles nodded. "Yeah."

Jesus looked me over. A TV squawked in another room and I pictured the pregnant tweeker on a chair in front of it, the racing heartbeats, colors playing across her face.

Jesus leaned over the bedside table to ash out his smoke and a grease stain marked his head's spot on the wall, and he said, "And you write for that newspaper?"

"The weekly."

"You should write about me, motherfucker," he said. "Make me a *star*."

"Not a bad idea," I heard myself say.

"I'm going to read your shit," he said. "See what kind of motherfucker you really are. What's your name?"

"Julian."

"Julian? Really yours, bro?"

I nodded.

"A wussy name."

"We're here to get some shit, if that's cool," Tinkles said. Tinkles spoke from desperation. He knew Jesus enough to know that the process of procuring speed from him needed to be pushed along, however gently.

We watched, waited. Speed jones and skin itches and a knife scraping wood. There was a pile of dirty clothes stuffed chest-high in the open closet, a rotary gun rack in the corner, and bouquets of scythed wires stuck out from gutted PCs on the room's edges. We stood there. An oscillating fan in one corner kept stench circulating. Iron Crosses of different sizes arranged altar-like atop a particleboard dresser with missing drawers inspired green on red images of racial dominance and soldiers disciplined with zero capacity for human warmth, and who were considered superior in every way. Jesus considered himself a soldier like that.

Heard a second woman above the TV noise in the other room. There were two back there, and a mess of indecipherable words. I could smell meth smoke.

"We could use an 8 ball," Tinkles said. "Hook us up?"

I hated that Jesus could reach out and unhook me. I hated his facial mullet and filthy feet and silly rebel-flag belt buckle. I hated Nazis. I hated tweekers and I hated me. I wanted the shit and the fuck out of there.

Time ticked and he told a story.

"My old man had been guzzling Blatz," Jesus said. "He always had a can of that shit in his hand. He was a tough motherfucker, ex-con, vet. But he never could get no decent job, so he did shit.

"One day there was pounding on the door. My old man hated unannounced visitors so he ignores the door and peeks through the curtains and goes for my baseball bat. The landlord just lets himself in. Now he ain't no average landlord neither. He was an old sweaty fuck of an ex-marine.

"Landlord says, 'You need to cough up some rent or get the fuck out.'"

Jesus resumed carving. The eye had shape.

"Ain't exactly what the old man wanted to hear," Jesus said. "So guess what he did next?"

"No idea," I said.

"He raised up that bat like Harmon Killebrew and the landlord just shook his head. Figured a hollow challenge. But it was no empty challenge. The old man swung that bat so hard into the old marine's skull his eyeball popped straight out."

"Jee-*sus*," I said. Wasn't thinking.

"That eye shot straight into the wall. And I'll be damned if our half-blind old dog didn't hop off the couch and lap up that bloody eyeball. The moan from the old man's maw was a whole other unholy. I was eight years old and I didn't sleep right for weeks."

He laughed and his entire body shook. He placed the knife and eye on the nightstand, sat back and lit a cigarette, and said, "So, the next thing I know we was living in a dirt-bag motel down off Van Buren."

There was a thump on the door.

Jesus instructed Tinkles to answer it. A skinny kid in a Ja Rule t-shirt holding a microwave burrito in one hand and a giant cup of Circle K coffee in the other. He looked 11. Said, "Will you give this to Jesus, please?"

Tinkles grabbed the concessions. "Wait," the kid said and reached into his pocket and drew out some cash and tucked it between Tinkles's forefinger and the coffee.

"For my mom," the kid said.

"Steve-O?" Jesus shouted from the bed.

"Yeah," the kid said.

"I got your mama covered." Jesus lowered his voice to Tinkles and said, "Bring that shit over here." Tinkles obeyed and placed the coffee, burrito and cash on the nightstand next to the lamp. Jesus counted the money. Yes he counted the money – he always counted the money – the money was his secret of success, such as it was. He leaned over and pulled a softball-sized fat sack from the nightstand drawer and opened it in his lap. It was packed with smaller baggies, each filled with varying amounts of translucent, rice-sized crystals. Thousands of dollars worth of narcotics and my stomach surged and my dick ached. We had to get it and go. Jesus slipped a baggie out, handed it to Tinkles, and said, "Give this to the kid."

Tinkles did as told. The kid thanked Jesus and Tinkles closed the door. Jesus placed the bindle of meth on the nightstand, ground his butt out in the ashtray there and picked up the knife and eye.

Then he shouted, "Lolly." Tinkles and I jumped. Jesus leaned over to see down the hallway. Again, louder and pissed, "Lolly!"

Lolly clicked up the hall and into the room. She was older than the one who'd greeted us and spindly in heels with over-bleached hair that looked to have stopped growing at her shoulders and was so thin it made her ears stand out. She stepped toward the bed and the lamplight shone on her face. I glanced at Tinkles to gauge his reaction to her face and he was just focused on the javelina hanging on the wall behind her. Wet dripped from his eyebrow.

Jesus nodded at Lolly, said, "She's my wife."

Jesus was showing how we weren't motherfucker enough to be in a room with him, prison-yard passive aggression. But I needed my meth. "Nice," I said, offering a hand to shake. "Good to meet you." That one eye looked through me. I pulled my hand back and Jesus smirked.

Lolly's face – I mean most of Lolly's face – was dipped in,

with two pig-snout holes in its center for breathing. Her top lip singed off above her gums, leaving an eternal smile highlighted by spaced apart teeth. She had no right eye, only a gluey patchwork of skin grafts, purple and yellow. She'd taken the time to apply makeup around her one eye — eyeliner, shadow, mascara.

In that moment she broke my heart. She knew too many ways to die but instead had accepted some way of living, and the makeup committed her to a kind of composure, or a sense of place in this world. Maybe the colors helped her dream of the girl she used to be and no amount of deformity could crush that. Lolly had waited half her life for someone to ruin her and Jesus was the one.

He nodded at her. Said, "That's yours. Leave a bulbie." Lolly pulled a filthy glass pipe from her pocket, placed it on the table and took the burrito and coffee.

"Needed somethin'," she said, and turned that smile at us, the one eye shooting between Tinkles and me like some mechanical aperture. Then she walked past us and was gone. Another ghost floating down that dark hallway.

"I seen meth make a friend chop his own brother's head off," Jesus said. "I seen it make the straight dude take it up the ass. I seen it make a mother fuck her son. But you need an eye for sin for that to happen. Eye for sin, like the Bible says."

He talked of Lolly losing all measure of sexual limitations on the shit, which is what happens. A reason why meth is so loved. Jesus said Lolly smoked it with their son.

"He was all of 15," Jesus said. "And then they started getting it on. I discovered that one day when I walked in and my son had his dick in her ass."

Jesus put the knife and eye on his stomach, reached to the

nightstand and slipped some meth from the bindle. He loaded the bulbed pipe, lit it, huffed hard and long, but didn't offer any. He exhaled, closed his eyes at the rush, and continued, "Then one day she got hold of some bad shit. That's what she called it. 'Bad shit.'"

He exchanged the pipe for the eye and knife. "But I snorted the same damn shit and I was fine. The doctors said the shit had larvae in it."

"Insect eggs in the meth?" I said.

Tinkles offered an attempt at levity: "Maybe health inspectors should go in and shut down those labs that have too many health violations, and present the certificates to the clean labs."

Jesus's expression showed total contempt. For some reason known only to Tinkles, Tinkles kept going: "You know, Crystal Meth Lab Health certification."

I chased a false laugh with a swig of the King. Jesus looked at Tinkles and shook his head. "She snorted it and she was *not* fine, Scottie. The larvae got all up in her head through her nose."

Jesus jerked forward, scowled. "Shit got all under her eyes." He drew imaginary lines on his cheekbone with the knife. "It went down along here and under her nose. Her face swelled up. The larvae metamorphosed in her face. You ain't seen nothin' like it."

"Christ," I said.

"Her skin was movin' slow like tiny baby puppies under a blanket. She figured it was a bad infection and kept doing the shit till she couldn't no more. Stupid woman."

"Fuck," I said.

"And you know what it was?"

I shook my head.

"Maggots," he said and leaned back against the wall, his head fitting the grease stain perfectly. "The fuckin' maggots multiplied, and she was going crazy from pain. I hauled her ass down to St. John's emergency."

"She survived at least," Tinkles said.

"You could call it that. The doctors excavated her face. Dug the fuckin' maggots out one at a time. Those little fuckers had burrowed in. Most of her face was eaten away."

Jesus waited for a response. None came and he said, "Woman lost her right eye. She hasn't left this house since the day she got home from the hospital. She only smokes the shit now." He paused a moment. Shook his head, and said, "But I love that woman beyond any mercy."

Whittling resumed. We waited. After some time he said, "If your eye causes you to sin, pluck it the fuck out."

We looked at each other at exactly the same moment, and his shirt armpits were soaked. He turned to Jesus. "Hey, can we get the shit now too? We need to go."

Jesus didn't respond but we did get to watch him smoke more meth. And carve. And carve some more.

Tinkles stammered.

Jesus responded with a sharp exhalation and a stream of hard-to-follow sentences and fucked-up non-sequiturs. I picked up bits involving stretches of jail time and tattoos honoring friends killed in Nam.

"Dude, you're too young to have fought in Vietnam," I said.

"Sixteen," Jesus said. "I looked older. Wasn't doin' nothin' but LSD to Zep and Sabbath. I was ready for war. My older brother, my only brother, got shot down over Laos on search and rescue. … My old man got murdered in '69. Mom had already checked out when my brother died. Drank herself dead. I wanted revenge, know what I mean? So I lied my way in, sayin' I was 18."

Jesus moved closer to the lamp and maneuvered his body to show tattoos on his back. "That's an AH-1W Super Cobra 'copter," he said pointing over his shoulder. "Armed with wing-mounted anti-tank missiles and a three-barrel Gatling gun that shoots 20-millimeter rounds. It could slice a dozen gooks in half at once, and it had the best avionics on any airborne. It's on my skin 'cause it saved my ass."

Bloody human bits decorated green foliage beneath the Cobra. Blood sprayed from necks of a couple of Yanks sprinting in fear, each with an outstretched arm, fingers spread, graphic-novel expressions of bug-eyed horror. Jesus reached around and his finger traced down along his lower spine, stretching the cowhide skin and tat.

"M14s, Marine issued," he said. "I couldn't save them two, my buds. Drinking buddies. One was a nigger but I loved him like a brother. Watched 'em both get ripped to shreds. Woke up screaming for two years after that." He settled back against the wall. "Good old Uncle Sam sends me disability, seven hundred, sixteen dollars and thirty-seven cents every month. Only good thing that ever came out of that war."

Sweat stung my eyes and dripped down my back. Jesus cranked it up: "I'm gonna show your asses somethin' real." He hopped up and moved to the gun rack in the corner. I'd forgotten how short he was, barely up to my chin. We could've murdered him right there, just punched him out and strangled him with our bare hands. Stranger shit has gone down in Sunnyslope.

"It's usually full," Jesus said pointing at the rack. "Have a few out."

One gun there reminded me of this guy I knew called Bolt.

He was injured during his shift at the Palo Verde nuke plant. His reward was a bum right leg and a large lump sum — enough to retire on and live out his days in semi-comfort. Boredom begat guns, and he soon owned automatics, semi-automatics, pistols, shotguns, grenades, even a flamethrower. One day he invited me shooting out in the desert. I'd never shot a gun before. I went along because who doesn't like to blow shit up? We got out there and he handed me a thirty-aught-six. I lifted it to my shoulder, aimed at something I can't remember and pulled the trigger. It thundered and I flew back onto my ass. Bolt howled. Couldn't move my right shoulder for a week and it was all black and blue. It was days before hearing returned to that side. Never shot again.

"I like the thirty-aught-six," I said.

He grinned. Black fissures framed piss-yellow teeth. "A gun for pussies."

Motherfucking goddammit. How long will this take?

Jesus fingers traced barrels and stopped on a silver shotgun.

"You need an over-under double barrel," he said, sliding the weapon up from the stand. He had meth shakes.

"Cool," I said.

Tinkles nodded. I knew he hated guns too.

"A Beretta 683 Gold E 12-gauge," Jesus said. "It's the monster of shotguns 'cause it's short, has easy sighting, weighs more and both barrels are stacked on top of each other instead of side by side."

Jesus bounced the shotgun gently between one hand and the other. "Perfect balance. I could cut you in half from a football field away."

He lifted it to his shoulder and aimed at the door. Then he lowered it, pressed a lever to the side and the barrels pivoted downward, revealing a pair of shotgun shells. "I keep it loaded," he said. He clicked the barrels back into place, returned the weapon to his shoulder and aimed it at the door again. He turned his upper body slowly and stopped so that the gun pointed at Tinkles' face.

Tinkles said, "Everythin' cool, Jesus?"

Jesus eased away from Tinkles and pointed the loaded shotgun at various spots around the room. He swung the gun around and slowly steadied his aim until it met that spot directly between my eyes. He kept it there. He squeezed an eye shut. I could see into the festering hate inside that one dilated pupil.

"It ain't easy to miss with one of these, son," he said pulling the lever back. I envisioned Tinkles covered in blood, sprinting away like those on Jesus's back.

Tinkles said, "Hey, Mayor. That's not really a good idea."

Good ol' Tinkles. Would've stepped in front of a bullet for me.

I mollified myself thinking of Scottie earning the name "Tinkles." Years ago we were at a house party and he'd passed out on the couch. Just a frizzy head poking up from some awful Starter jacket with dirty work slacks and slimy shoes, all laid out cold in front of everyone — the beautiful girls and dudes from shitty bands, the affected hipsters and asshole coke heads, all of 'em. Soon enough it became obvious that he'd pissed himself; his pants, from crotch to knees, were saturated. And they all laughed, even the girls. Some laughed convulsively. They threw beer on him, tampons, and doused him with detergent. It was horrible. I managed to get him out of there and home to his bed.

His problem worsened. He'd piss himself whenever he drank to oblivion, which was nightly. But it wasn't just the drinking that exacerbated his condition. No, Tinkles was one dude who always managed to maintain some shitty full-time job. Forever working in fast food explained his corpulence and bragging that he ate free. So between the drinking – which, when you figure in hangovers and recovery time, could be a fulltime gig – and his actual paying job as a Burger King assistant manager, he never had time, much less inkling, to shower. He'd often pass out in his work clothes and piss. Then he'd get up and go to work in the very same clothes because by then the pants would be dry. The piss and sweat and meat and French fry grease and, oh, *dear god*.

But then, on the night of his 22nd birthday, everything changed. The night he took control of his bladder. There was a girl, Jamy or someone. She lasted a week in his life, but he'd changed in that week. He never wet himself again. Poor Tinkles only needed a woman's touch.

———————

Jesus's right eye twitch spread to his mouth and cheek. "It makes me sick how the kids act like the rapper niggers," he said.

"What?" I said.

"Aryan kids thinkin' they're ghetto niggers. ..."

The horseshit sermon droned. You can't reason with hate, especially tweeker hate. I blocked it out. Saw my mother smoking a cigarette and dancing around a record player to Johnny Nash singing "I Can See Clearly Now," a face full of contented joy that no husband or child could corrupt.

I couldn't take Jesus another second. I said, "Every idiot knows Africa is the fucking birthplace of all humanity."

Total silence.

I stared into the barrels waiting for the concussion. I wondered what it would look like. A big wet rose on my shoulders?

His jaw jutted forward, twitching worsened, eye narrowed. Cockeyed obscenities sputtered out, low at first. "Arrrghhgorrra buh-buh."

Then out erupted a shudder-inducing tweeker's Tourette's, bullhorn-loud: "Cunt. Jizz-gurgling … arrrghhgorrra buh-buh bitch a kickluntass … " Every hard consonant jerked his body as if it was seized by something wretching "… Cunt! … Fuck! …"

Tinkles had once warned of Jesus's occasional "wig outs." The TV volume in the other room went way up, the ritualized action of an insane household.

Jesus: "Cunt … Fuck … Lickluntass … "

Then Tinkles snapped. Just like that. I watched gape-jawed his 240-pound frame sail over the edge of Jesus's bed, arm and fingers out-stretching mid-air and snatching the happy sack of meth off the nightstand, sending the lamp, fake eye and knife crashing to the floor. He bounced off the bed shouting "run!" but lost balance and shot headlong into the door. But he was up instantly, hobbling frantically into the night. I followed three steps back.

Halfway to the Corolla I realized I was still holding Jesus's quart of Bud. I stopped and thought that for once in my life maybe a succession of shitty choices needn't be compounded by one more shitty choice and that maybe I had a chance at something other than *this*. That pit bull had opened up again. I felt guilty stealing from Jesus. Hell, Jesus probably needed the beer. I rushed back and peeked inside the open door. Jesus and shotgun hadn't moved, his jaw gnawed, "Arrrghhgorrra … arrrghhgorrra buh-buh bitch …" I leaned in slightly, placed the beer inside the door and sprinted to the car. I jumped in and Tinkles opened up that throttle. A pair of dead dudes hauling out of there.

The joy could barely be contained inside soft internal blossoms. We were Supermen.

"Dude," I said. "That's the bravest thing you've ever done."

Tinkles grinned wide. He reached into the bindle and slipped out a little baggie. I took it, killed the air conditioning, and dumped half of it on a CD jewel case, one of many scattered inside the car. I used a cigarette lighter to crush the crystals and divvy up a pair of thick lines. I found an old Big Gulp straw on the floor, stuck it in my mouth and burned it in half with the lighter. I balanced the CD case with one hand while Tinkles drove very gently and I blew on the straw until the melted part was dry. I stuck one end in a nostril and hard-snorted a thick one deep into my head. I sucked it back again, hard — burn, sting, hiss, elation. I held the CD case under Tinkles' nose with one hand and handed him the straw and took the wheel with the other. He snorted the crank up, spluttered and shook his head. We each slipped into our quiet, heart-pounding realms of infinite potentials.

He tucked the bag of speed safely under his seat and flipped on the air. I rolled down my window and Tinkles eased that beat Corolla into Northwest Phoenix as the sun began to show its edges and suck the entire world into its unyielding arms. Acres of ranch-style homes subdivided on irrigated land hogged our sightlines, acres that years ago were citrus groves. The smell of freshly cut lawns, and the orange, lemon and grapefruit blossoms reminded me of springtime mornings between home and school just before summer break. There was still plenty of hanging fruit, in the backyards, on the lawns, along the roadside. All you had to do was stop. All the life-giving fruit you could ever dream of.

No Wheels

No Wheels

The store clerks were a slight irritation. Joe, Raul and Stanley all worked evenings and nights at a Circle K convenience store, usually on different days, and I'd see them so often I knew them by name, and then some. For example, I knew Joe was working his way up to Circle K manager. He should be there in a year. Raul lived just a few streets over on Fillmore, and he walked to work. He lived in absolute poverty because he supported three kids, a wife and a mother-in-law, all on a Circle K wage. Stanley lived nearby too. I knew that Stanley's wife weighed in at 300 pounds and that Raul's wasn't much lighter. Often I'd overhear Stanley bitching to Joe or Raul about his wife's fondness for Circle K's rotisserie weiners, big bags of Doritos and anything grape flavored, and over the months that I'd frequented that particular Circle K, he started telling me things about her too. Like how her weight problems guaranteed a disability that led directly to government checks, which, while easing their financial woes considerably, also led to her bad, day-long TV habit and, Stanley explained, more recent problems involving her health, none of which could overcome the fact that, he made a point to say, her ginormous tits made his life worth living.

I learned too that Stanley's wife could go up to six days without a single bowel movement. That chunk of info stuck with me longer than anything else I knew of Stanley, his wife, or Circle K in general. I happened to see her once outside the store, arguing with Stanley during one of his smoke breaks. She wore a too-snug poly top. Yes, she weighed at least 300 pounds. Stanley was on the thin side, and the two of them together looked like a palm tree next to a three-story house. All I could think when I saw her was when was the last time she'd had a bowel movement?

After two months of regular visits to the Circle K, Joe, Raul and Stanley had all started to comment on how much malt liquor I consumed. The comments made me self-conscious. Though they were cool about it, because I'd gotten to know them somewhat, they still felt compelled to say that they couldn't believe how much malt liquor I could drink. Because of that, I began alternating my beer purchases between three different stores, all within walking distance. Other than the Circle K, I'd hit Ajax Wine Castle and A-1 Beer and Spirits, which were located down Van Buren, east of 16th Street.

The two liquor stores were similar. Each smelled of pipe tobacco, though A-1 smelled mostly of dogs too. Each had a massive wall of crappy and top-shelf booze behind the counter, the whiskey, vodka, scotch, bourbon and rum. You had to ask for that stuff like you do cigarettes and cigars. Wine was shelved out on the floor among the racks of leafed-through porn magazines and Cheetos, and the beer was kept in coolers. Bear paw bolo ties and bootleg Arizona Diamondback t-shirts were available near the register, and you could choose from an array of boner supplements and smoking paraphernalia. There was always classic rock or country going at low volume.

I could purchase forties here quietly. There was no commentary like that from the Circle K guys. The cashiers at the liquor stores were older, jaded, and had tats that showed they did time as inmates and soldiers. They rarely budged from their elevated posts behind the registers and often stared blankly at Diamondback games on a little TV, but sometimes I'd detect in their eyes that they had an understanding of what I understood, and that drinking soothed that understanding. Like I could be their friend but that friendship would have to be earned because there was a sense of mutual anonymity and it outweighed any desires, or perhaps abilities, to actually connect. It was just atmospheric comfort, and conversation was never more than what I owed and did I want a bag? I told myself that these guys saw me as a notch above the other drunks who frequented the place. I told myself that and it made me feel better. I wanted their respect.

But it had a price. The beer at the liquor store was about 20 percent pricier than at Circle K. That's roughly forty cents more for a forty of King Cobra. The price difference was how they kept some riff-raff out. It's how they kept me out too because sometimes I just didn't have the extra coin. I'd also get cornered by any number of street urchins whose whole lives played out on the sidewalks outside the liquor stores. There was this one huge homeless alchy everyone knew as Stud 'n' Suds. He walked tall with a strident sense of sidewalk ownership. He had yellowy, bloodshot eyes that some days showed kindness. On others they could be filled with hatred and avarice. One day Stud 'n' Suds was wearing a cowboy hat and a vintage B-52s t-shirt. I'd never seen a giant black guy wearing a B-52s t-shirt. I told him I dug his Goodwill score. From that day on he'd glom on to me whenever he'd see me. He'd tell me that he was an informant for the Phoenix P.D. and that they were onto me. Said he'd clear my name with the cops for a ten spot. He said that every time I'd see him, and every time I'd get paranoid and head home at a faster clip than when I left. For weeks he didn't change out of that B-52s t-shirt. It turned rank, discolored. Then he was gone.

It was impossible to remain anonymous at Circle K because the employees seemed to remember me. Maybe the survey methodology employed by the Circle K cashiers correlated directly with the marketing of the beer because they'd often point out, as if I was unaware, that I was the only white dude who ever purchased malt liquor at their store. Maybe that was the tip: I was the only gringo purchasing forties of King Cobra.

I loved The King. See, a forty-ounce King Cobra was cheap, a buck ninety-six with tax, and it filled you up, especially if you were starving. Its metallic aftertaste resembled Budweiser but with a bitterer edge, and double the kick, as it contained more alcohol. It has menace. Your average beer is mainly made up of barley, hops and water. Your two-buck forties of malt liquor have higher ratios of fermentable sugars. That means it's not meant for leisurely drinking. It also gets swampy pretty fast, so it's best to drink quickly, and finish while it's still cold. I'd make forties last about 45 minutes.

Half the fun of malt liquor, or any beer, was the walk up to the store to get it. I looked forward to that nearly as much as I did the beer itself. I'd wait for that horrible sun to descend into that dirty-orange panorama behind the Phoenix skyline before heading out. Best time. That hour before the night lights up. That's when the heat waned and the neighborhood edges softened. From my place, I'd stroll west down Polk Street to 11th and cut over to my Circle K. A mile and a half round trip.

Now this Circle K was life among the dead, which is why it was my favorite place to go and buy beer. It was the quick fix in a neighborhood where there were no outs. At night its bright fluorescent lights reached out to the middle of Van Buren, offering hope for late-night transience, for the lonely and the reclusive. Hope for the meth-addled prostitutes I'd see whose bodies were long past reclamation, and for the desert-rat day-workers with shot, red eyes who'd stammer through the bell-ringing doors and nod with glee upon discovering that they'd made it before the 1 a.m. cut-off time to purchase Bud Light. It was light for those like me who were taken in by the smell of burnt dogs and fresh coffee and the promise of ice-cold malt liquor, and the existence of at least one other late-night human being. Light for those like me who were just becoming aware that they were speeding on some road to the bottom and not even listening to what their own story might or might not have been telling them.

The Circle K ornamented a neighborhood lined with flimsy houses and indignant dwellings. Lots of mottled stucco and crudely erected rooms made of rusting tin, some held together with bailing wire and putty, and swamp coolers chugged and leaked atop low roofs. Zoning laws didn't apply here. It was as if any city land-use planning had been grandfathered in from a time long ago that no one can remember. That, and nobody cared. Mean rangy dogs roamed and barked holy hell, and sometimes it was a challenge not to get chased. If I spotted one when too far from home I'd step carefully, avoid any eye contact, or stop altogether and wait for him to move on and be prepared to sprint like a motherfucker if he came at me. I counted lucky stars that I never got mauled by one of those bastards. But not everyone can survive in the Garfield barrio.

The street held other anomalies, including a fading three-story Spanish revival mansion from the early 1900s. A copper-mining baron had built the thing as a wedding gift for his daughter. It became a whorehouse at one point. Now it's a state-funded home for battered women. The assholes always put the women's shelters in the worst areas of Phoenix. It had a broad, wraparound porch and arched windows and doors. It was sun-beaten into the color of dirt, surrounded by a man-tall wrought-iron fence, which was gated and chain-locked and topped with strands of barbed wire. I'd see women on the porch sometimes, standing in the strange Arizona-long shadows, silent and hunched over, older than their bones, and cornered. Hispanic, Native American, black, or squat in pregnancy, or thin as hope.

The place had a rich, tended-to garden, which was a whole other wonder to me. How did they get tomatoes and peppers and cucumbers to grow here?

I'd pass lovely Our Lady of Guadalupe grottos, three on my walk. Each was set in a chain-linked yard of hard dirt and sagebrush. I'd tell myself that these Virgin Marys were too graceful to surrender to the heat. They soothed in cyan and magenta, in rosaries and beeswax. They provided a few square feet of guilt and reclamation, particularly on the return walk, when it was dark and after I'd downed some beer. Sundown always triggered that need to crack the day's first beer. Alcohol beautified the transition from ugly day into beautiful evening. The crooked power lines and untrimmed palm trees stood quiet guard on the suddenly restive streets, which stretched into darkness lit on both sides by porches and living rooms.

As it got dark I'd smell fried masa or beef cooked in cumin and oregano, see dads guzzling Bud Light on hoods of

American heaps, and hear Tejano and Norteño faves blaring from too-loud Salvation Army blasters. Sometimes night breezes would be hot enough I'd envision wildfires whipping up through desert arroyos, way out beyond the city limits, and I'd squint into flames the radio towers atop South Mountain.

My Mexican casita was one of seven situated back off the street around an unpaved patio in a mesquite, cacti and Palo Verde oasis. The bungalows housed the only non-Latinos in the neighborhood, and each inhabitant was a drunk, except the landlord, Ira. Ira was a Phoenix ghetto land baron, a dude of 60 who also owned a tai chi studio just west of downtown. I loved Ira because he was honest, and sometimes altruistic. He'd help folks out. He'd rescue outcall hookers by pulling them out of shitty situations. Then he'd move them into one of his bungalows. He'd feed them (and their kids), and then, after a number of weeks, he'd start fucking them. Ira never wanted to fuck them, he'd tell me, it would "just happen." I believed that he never really wanted to fuck them because once he did he'd wear his guilt. You'd see it. He'd walk with a slouch, as if gravity was pulling his shoulders slightly inward and down. That stoop would creep into his posture every time he'd start sleeping with a new girl. The women and their children would come and go. When they'd move out Ira would begin walking upright again.

Ira had the most beautiful bungalow too. Restored plaster walls, lots of antiquated furniture with feminine curves, old rugs he shipped back from his trips to Mozambique and Turkey. He saw beauty in rusted wheelbarrows and rescued palms and found objects and knew exactly where to place them all. The drunks just trampled over all the beauty there.

The bungalows were bordered by dispirited stretches of duplexes, all of which were inhabited, and had electricity, despite the windows being boarded-up. Overfull trashcans on the porch spilled dead Bud Light cans out into the street, and at night interior lights slanted through the busted up plywood and round faces emerged on dark porches.

Lots of undocumented immigrants would come and go from these duplexes, and there'd be new faces every other week. They stayed fed and amused with little coin and often let out real joy in the nights, and you'd hear it, feel it, for hours. Lots of mad waltz-timed anthems sung in Spanish. Rarely were women around those places and the dudes would laugh and drink and shout shit at me like *"Maricón, maricón!"* and *"dar por el culo."* I might as well have been from Uranus. Hell, I'd laugh at me too: all hungover under a rat's-nest of unwashed hair, a backdated dreamer with a headful of Henry Miller and old T. Rex. The Latinos were too drunk to follow up the name-calling, and they'd never step off their porches to start a fight; they'd never do anything to draw cops and I figured most had mothers to answer to. Good Catholic sons at the end of the day. Good thing too because I didn't know how to fight. But I'd be envious of their joy.

I saw big families too on my Polk Street, and immigrants from El Salvador, Chile, Ecuador or Mexico, who lived and laughed and drank, struggled to just be, in a city on a land of the free where they're judged, hated. Where they work horrible day-laborer jobs as garbage removers, landscapers and roofers over long hours in insufferable heat, earning little money.

―――――――――

Of all the Circle K cashiers, I liked Raul the best. He was gentle but you could tell he was hurting somehow. One night when I was in purchasing smokes and beer he asked if he could come over sometime and drink a beer. I said sure, though I didn't really want him to, and I didn't think he would. Few things are ever followed up on in my life. Also, I'm not the biggest fan of houseguests and I like to keep acquaintances at arm's length. But he did come by, on foot, and it wasn't bad. We talked and drank out on my porch until about midnight and then he left.

Then Raul began to stop by a couple times a week, usually in the late evening after his Circle K shift was over. He'd be tired from working on his feet for nine hours. He'd bring along a forty of King Cobra (for me) and a 12-pack of Keystone, which I'd enjoy after killing off the forty.

One night he came by and we went to the street and sat on the curb. He cracked my King Cobra and handed it to me and then he cracked a Keystone for himself. It was obvious that Raul had had it. Then he got all teary-eyed, which was uncomfortable as hell.

"Julian?" he said. "What do you do with three kids?"

"I don't know, man," I said.

"What do you do with a wife who hates you, and you hate her?"

"I don't know the answer to that one either. I had a wife but that didn't end well at all."

"Did you have kids?" he asked.

"Nope."

"Lucky."

After some time he said, "How do you live with a mother-in-law who you hate?

"Got me."

"Do we learn to like ourselves?"

I just shook my head.

Some kid about 12 years old rode by on a chop-shopped bike that squeaked but looked badass. It had brand-new parts and others that were pounded into place. It sported out-stretched forks and a gnarly green-sparkled banana seat, a double-tall sissybar, a bullet headlight, a rainbow of reflectors and down-turned stingray bars slung so low that the driver's back was horizontal to the street and his face was about three feet from it as he pedaled. Whole thing resembled a lunar-rover some science fiction writer might've dreamed up in 1953. His younger sister followed in vain on her pink trike, face squinched in determination, handlebar streamers, shoulders pushing forward with each pedal stroke — hard left, hard right — overcoming drag from half-flat tires. They looked happy as hell.

We watched the little parade pass us by. We watched them roll up the street into the dark, turn around and then ride by again. We drank from our beers.

Raul said, "Man, this just isn't going to work. I have a car payment and rent and three kids and a wife and a mother-in-law."

I nodded. I felt for Raul. He really was a good dude. It's easy to get cornered in a city like Phoenix. You're especially lost if you don't have a car, or if you don't have a real job, much less a career. I didn't have any of those things.

Folks flock to Phoenix because there's money here, and lots of it. It's a city heavily populated by fleshy white people with gluttonous ambitions who drive around in brand new cars that cost more than what my bungalow would sell for. They fear brown skin and live in gated communities and vote Republican. Their own skin rarely touches sunshine or wind. They move from an air-conditioned residence to an enclosed garage to their air-conditioned cars to underground parking garages to air-conditioned buildings. I always figured that if you don't feel the elements, you shut down inside. But what do I know? Our bungalows had swamp boxes for cooling, which did little more than blow hot, humid air and make things damp and moldy. And if it rained, forget it; the humidity was unbearable.

Raul got me thinking about my own various mental damages. I realized that I at least had a couple of buffers. For example, I had a girlfriend out in Tempe who owned a car and had a real job. Sometimes when I was hungry and broke she'd bring me beer and burritos. I had no kids and no responsibilities except for whatever little writing deadlines or gigs with my band, which was floundering. But I often felt like I was trapped at the bottom of a slimy dark well. I was really only happy once the sun went down and the beer was flowing.

Raul and me were very much alike. We had zero chance of ever becoming one of those people whom others respected and admired. We'd never make it as software developers or phlebotomists or scouts for the Arizona Cardinals. But I was nowhere near as cornered as Raul, and that made me feel guilty when I was around him. My responsibilities amounted to this: I had one key, the one that unlocked my front and back door. My mailbox was broken so it didn't lock, so I didn't need a key for that. Because I'd lost the one key so many times, I'd taken to wearing the thing around my neck on a shoestring. The shoestring-key idea was my girlfriend's. She was just so exasperated at me being locked out time and again. She always said I was a 12-year-old who had managed to gain decades of experience. I needed her but she didn't need me. Not good.

Raul and I sat there on the curb drinking our beer. We watched a group of weird little desert bats psychotically circle the one streetlight that wasn't shot out, and the brother-sister bike team paraded by again.

"Want a smoke?" he said.

We smoked on the curb and worked on our beer.

"Do you smoke much?" He said.

"Trying to stop. But I don't know why I'd even try. It's like trying to stop drinking. There's no real reason to."

"Right," Raul said. "My wife hates my drinking."

"That's tough."

"Right. And my middle daughter, who turns eight this week, is autistic."

I shook my head. We were both quiet for a while.

Two dudes drinking beer out on a curb was another dude's invite to join. So my neighbor Frank walked over and stood next to us but faced the street. He wore khaki shorts with flip-flops and carried an Old Milwaukee. Frank was a short-fingered drunk of about 35, skinny but with an expanding paunch, and he never wore a shirt, day or night, which meant he was tan, and red-faced as all hell. He told me once that he averaged between 27 and 30 Old Milwaukees a day.

"Frank, this is Raul," I said. "Raul, this is Frank."

"Hey, man," Raul said. Frank nodded and chugged from his beer.

All three of us stayed quiet.

Frank was a smart guy. He spoke German and Spanish and a polyglot of Chinese, Korean and Japanese. Grew up on Air Force bases. But like some of the others in the bungalows, he had dropped out of something, or was hiding out from someone, or was just damaged in some way. Pretty sure Frank was all three of those things. He'd earned an MBA from Columbia. He never talked much about how he'd pissed away his marriage and six-figure job. He'd been arrested for some DUIs back in Florida, made bail and wound up down in a Phoenix barrio. He'd been shacking up with another drunk, the manly, boxy-shaped Dinora, a vodka-drip Latina. Dinora had a city job, cleaned up animal feces at the zoo. It surprised the hell out of everyone in the bungalows when Frank moved in with her because we thought for sure she only liked women. She only ever talked about women. I liked that about her. Testosterone ruins everything. Every now and then she'd have a woman friend over. We'd see them through Dinora's front window enjoying a candlelit dinner. Then they'd get drunk and slow dance to old Emmylou Harris records on the front porch.

Frank and Dinora would drink and then fight. One night a few months before they'd gotten into it worse than usual, Dinora heaved Frank's prized model airplane through her open front window. It flew over the porch and crashed into their concrete birdbath, the same birdbath the two of them drunkenly carried home one night after abducting it from some old house in the neighborhood. The model was a Messerschmitt Bf 109 WWII fighter. It had a three-foot wingspan. Frank spent months detailing the thing just so. He'd often talk about the hours of work he put into it, how he'd research the plane at the library to get the era's colors and tone just right. Like I said, he spent months on the thing. He was proud of it.

The Messerschmitt exploded into a hundred pieces when it hit the birdbath. Frank was shattered.

The very next day I watched from my porch as Frank moved his love seat, the one patterned like '80s golf pants, a stained mattress, piles of half-mutilated books, and a couple boxes worth of shit into a vacant bungalow on the far side of the courtyard. The landlord had a vacancy, which was very convenient for Frank. Didn't even have to change his address.

But since he'd moved, an invisible line of demarcation appeared through the yard that neither Frank nor Dinora would cross.

Anyway, Dinora started banging this big Canadian dude named Logan. I swear I saw him hanging around the courtyard just before she smashed up Frank's Messerschmitt. Logan had to be at least 50, and he patrolled the dirt courtyard barefoot, wearing only boxers, like some kind of soused soldier. He'd talk of his days as a winning boxer and how he was still an esteemed member of the Canadian Amateur Boxing Federation. He had a full head of neck-length strawberry-blond hair with wisps of gray, and crazy, unblinking eyes. He was tan and tall with a distended gut, had flabby arms, a gold chain and a big red nose. He showed up seemingly out of nowhere with a rotted grin talking about rectal cocaine and Ernest Hemingway and his daughter who just entered college in Vancouver. He shacked right up with Dinora only hours after Frank had moved out. Just like that.

Logan drank beer all day and then at sundown retired to an aluminum lawn chair up on their porch. He was by then blind drunk and shouting shit. If he'd see me in the courtyard he'd call me names. "Footless faggot" was the one that stuck. If I made eye contact with him he'd psychically attack me and because his gaze was so psychotic it was hard to look away. And if I stepped any closer, or away, he'd warn of his "patented" left hook. It was like getting trapped by one of the hood dogs. One night Frank was on the receiving end of that "patented" left hook and it wasn't pretty. It took a week for him to regain sight in his busted right eye but that eyelid forever drooped.

By six p.m. Dinora would be home from work and hitting the Smirnoff. By nine o'clock they'd be arguing a shitstorm about anything, like proper torque on wheel bearings, or Rush versus

REO Speedwagon, or frostbacks verses wetbacks, and so on. By 10 p.m. their words would be indecipherable, screened in spittle, and, by 11 p.m., they'd be passed out in their chairs, side by side. Frank and Dinora used to do the same damn thing. True love.

Frank owned a car and he worked four days a week walking dogs for rich people. He made a habit of saying that he couldn't be happier. Because he thought himself to be some kind of spiritual wellspring his beliefs encompassed a variety of traditions, namely those that lifted him into rarified air. He talked of things he'd picked up while backpacking through Southeast Asia, and then in Mexico, and he could quote from English translations of Mahāvastu texts until the cows came home, but, really, from what I saw, he was only happy drunk. When he was sober he'd have that alcoholic scowl face, and his scowl face was getting more pronounced as the months went by. He became slightly beady-eyed as the alcohol bloat filled in his cheekbones and widened his beard, which sometimes showed dime-sized bits of day-old vomit.

Raul welcomed Frank. Raul was a nice, trusting guy.

When Frank appeared I was attempting to cheer up Raul. I told him there are much worse places to be employed than at a Circle K.

After nine years of employment Raul had become entombed at Circle K. He was promoted once, to some kind of managerial position, though he'd been stuck up at gunpoint at least a dozen times. He said he stopped keeping track years ago of how many times he'd been robbed at the store, just as he'd lost count of the employees who had walked out or been fired.

And Raul worked harder than any person I knew. I watched him work. It was the worst kind of job because it was often dull and he was always dealing with customers, a good percentage of whom were unruly or indigent or preteen. He'd take great care when escorting the homeless out of the store, and looked the other way if they stuffed food in their pockets. His long list of hourly duties included everything from making coffee and keeping the donut area clean, to ensuring the shelves and coolers were stocked and orderly, and that the beer cooler, which drew the heaviest traffic, was always organized. Every few hours he'd wipe the front doors of hand grease and once a day he'd mop the place. His managerial post meant he oversaw a lot, such as the gas pumps, and cash registers. He once told me that if a register came up short on his clock they'd dock his pay or fire him. He lived in fear of that. Comforting reward for years of service.

"It's hard work because Circle K is the hood's lifeblood," I told him. "Think of it. There'd be nothing in this part of town but two shitty liquor stores. You work at the one place that's safe, well lit, and offers toilet paper and borderline legitimate food.

"Raul," I continued, "you work more hours, and harder in those hours, than anyone I know."

"Yes," Raul said. "So? Fifty hours a week to stay in the same place. I used to come home at night thinking I did a difficult day's work for my family. But I don't think like that now. I think that I am a failure."

Frank chimed in. "It's a very American ideal that says you fail because you are a pussy. It's a load of horseshit, of course."

"True," I said. "Also, hard work doesn't necessarily get you anywhere."

"We can work our asses off for years and still nose-dive," Frank added. "I've done it."

"Me too," I said. "And we all want some fucking meaning in our lives. And who wants to believe that all the shit we deal with is determined by people — such as your Circle K Corporation, Raul — kicking us around?"

"I'd say it's good on a personal level to believe that we are mostly in control of our destinies," Frank said. "That's supposed to make us work harder. But that too is a load of horseshit. Also, you'll never make it on a service wage. Not in this country."

Raul nodded in agreement and drank from his beer.

"I have yet to meet a successful person who made it by not breaking the rules," Frank added. "Yet we're supposed to abide by those rules. It's no wonder our culture creates so many homeless drunks."

I raised a toast to that. Frank and Raul joined me.

Then Raul said, again, but this time to Frank, "So how do you live with a wife that you hate?"

Frank said, "You take that hate and tell yourself you're just reliving some hateful episode from younger days. It's not hate. It's love. You just get tired."

"So you're tired, Frank?" I said.

My comment annoyed Frank and he shook his head deliberately. Frank was easily annoyed. He said, "Listen, the kind of tired that I'm talking about is only destruction in life. We don't exist beyond the present moment. Might as well make the best of it by not judging it."

Frank was swaying back and forth in place as if riding upright in a public bus. That's how you knew he was drunk. Frank was one of those weirdoes who could get completely sloshed but never slur a word. That and he took to lecturing you when he was drunk, which made everything he said an absolute bore. Frank got so serious when he was sloshed I learned to avoid any sarcasm around him. One crack and he'd inevitably point out how he lived in an evolved state, in his own private irony-free bubble. Said irony was refuge for anyone too chickenshit to be truly honest. Frank could make a good point, I suppose, but he took it too far. A person needs something to laugh at, even the absurdities of daily living.

"Was it love when Dinora heaved your ME-109 and it blew up into a million pieces?" I said. Couldn't help it.

Frank thought about that one. Rocked back and forth some, and said, "Yes, it was. Her way of kindness."

Just then I heard Dinora shuffling up in flip-flops. I turned and watched her thick calves and bruised ankles move closer. The straps of her purple sundress cut two mountain roads into her fleshy shoulders. She carried a mason jar half-filled of clear liquid with minimal ice and a floating slice of lime. She was pretty hammered.

Standing behind Raul and me, she said, "So this is where the party's at?"

No one said anything.

Then Dinora turned to Frank, pointed at him with her drink, and said, "I see you've invited the world's greatest jizz-toss to your event."

I looked over at Frank. He was riding that bus, but his gaze focused down on the dirt.

She added, "Wouldn't it be fucking hilarious if Satan looked just like you?"

Raul cracked a fresh Keystone, as if to punctuate Dinora's comment and ensuing silence. Frank sipped once from his Old Milwaukee and lifted his chin some. Dinora sneered. Raul made a frightened face at me.

Logan was off in the courtyard somewhere quarrelling with himself at a pretty good volume. I had introduced him to King Cobra a couple days before.

Frank turned his drooped glare to me for a long moment as if to confide a thank you for introducing Logan to malt liquor. Then he pressed his lips together, nodded his head and turned and walked away in short little-kid steps, flip-flops leaving baby clouds of dust in the dirt.

Dinora looked at us for a short moment and Raul dropped his eyes in shame. I averted my gaze too because I couldn't think of a lie. Then she turned and went back in the general direction of Logan's theater.

Raul looked at me. "What's with them?"

"True love," I said.

Raul said, "Maybe that Frank does have shit figured out?"

"When you get right down to it."

We sipped our beers and stayed silent for a long while.

Ira slipped through the trees from the direction of his bungalow carrying a full, twist-tied plastic trash bag. He was walking toward the trashcans that lined the curb on the street. He was walking with a pretty good slouch.

The Delivery Man

The Delivery Man

Little winged fuckers shooting sonic fuck-yous through brick and drywall. Dog-day cicadas, all right. Sounded like hydraulic wrenches removing lug nuts. Morning sun crammed cracks between the blankets and sheets tacked up over the bedroom windows, and I was nude, sticky-wet to the mattress, making starfish of dust particles swirling in slivers of sunlight. Hair hurt too, heart kicked inside eyeballs and skin sweated malt liquor and crystal meth.

The TV beamed porn down upon us from its wobbly perch atop boxes stacked at the foot of the bed and the anatomy of others played across our own salty skin. The third day of a sleepless broil, and the endless supply of porno owned us still. Serena's masturbating sounded vaguely like water shoaling sand and I drifted into it. Saw myself in cool saltwater on the Santa Monica beach, the gently spraying spume and clipping light, and walking out on it, wide-eyed and straight into the sun. She had to be ready to die. I was, if I wasn't dead already.

I had to piss. I stood and the temples hammered and I nearly fainted. Go steady man; breathe. I stepped over the porn DVD boxes and empty King Cobra bottles and made it to the toilet and let it out. Then I examined myself in the full-length mirror.

The recent weight loss had been something – stomach concave, elbows sharp, cheekbones high, shoulder blades protruding; I was down thirty from my buck-fifty average. I straightened up, turned to one side and then the other. I imagined celebrity skin and squinted myself into a naked runway model sucker-punched by a gnarly coke addiction. I saw other things, like the startled ghost of my future self with a face carved mercilessly into canyons and gulches by the little Toxin River hidden in the darkness between folds of skin, a face internally abused beyond any reasonable recognition.

I used the towel slung over the shower curtain rod to wipe wet from my face and neck, and leaned into the mirror for a closer look. Blotches of busted blood vessels – the telltale signs of a Swiss-cheesing liver – shaped the two shittiest states: Florida ran the length of my nose and Ohio sat beneath my left eye. Sore nostrils, pinkish and translucent, mouth chafed raw. I zeroed in on a deep-rooted blackhead between my nose and cheekbone and squeezed hard.

From the other room the porno sounded like funeral bereavement, and the weight of untold personal terrors swelled and gained steam. Descending.

Back in the bedroom I chugged a flat, half-full forty of King Cobra and felt a bit better. Serena was upright in bed, using a razorblade to chop meth on a CD case that showed four Ramones with their backs against the wall. *Rocket to Russia*. The butterfly between her breasts glistened and Johnny Ramone began riffing in my ears. A strident wall of distorted downstrokes turned into astral harmonic freakout, which grew louder until Johnny's spiritual brudda Joey appeared before me, all lanky with an arm outstretched toward my face, forefinger pointed upward, a homoerotic come-hither, a double-chin and small pink mouth, singing: *Slugs and snails are after me/DDT keeps me happy/Now I guess I have to tell 'em/That I got no cerebellum …*

It had gotten to that point that I'd taste meth, see butterfly tats and hear Ramones riffs whenever I saw Serena sober, before she spread herself open and before we'd even scored the drugs. And Serena was all about The Ramones, all the time. Early Ramones: the first five albums. Her co-workers at The Bush Cabin nude bar all stripped to Guns N' Roses, Marilyn Manson and Jay Z. Not Serena. Ramones, man. She was a baby when the Ramones were great but she knew everything about them. She'd argue how they'd lost it after Phil Spector manhandled them, as if anyone at her work had ever heard of Phil Spector.

I once watched Serena writhe down to her knee-highs as the Ramones' semi-tender "I Want You Around" pumped through the club's sound system. In her eyes I saw light to be lost in forever. On the nude-dancer stage, in a roomful of ugly, classic-rock rednecks, in a city that had no real spirit for anything, she wore it all without effort. Was as willowy and finely tuned as a swan on a filthy lake. She still earned forty bucks on a Ramones song that I guarantee everybody in that joint hated but me. It jump-started my wretched little alcoholic heart.

The Ramones vanished when Serena said, "We're running low." Her hand tremors, a byproduct of consuming meth and beer for days and skipping food and sleep, nearly caused the shit to spill to the bed and floor.

"Watch the fuck out!" I said.

"Fuck snorting," she said. "We *need* to smoke it. Go grab my bag."

I was never a fan of smoking, and I hated needles. I always snorted.

Yes, each snorted line sears the thin skin and cartilage of your nasal septum and you instantly taste the slag and toilet cleaner, or whatever it is, drip down your throat, but it's somehow less noxious than with a pipe or needle, so you actually feel like you'll live a little longer, even when you don't really want to. Seemed more acceptable when you snorted too, like how your parents might've snorted blow at parties. Every idiot did coke in bathrooms and kitchens. Christ, it was like drinking.

Smoking it singed your face and blistered your lungs, tongue and lips. Tasted like leaky batteries. And that was just in the beginning. The upside was you got more for your money by shooting or smoking it, and early hits were like fighter jets bursting sound barriers inside your skull.

But shooting it really tripped my guilt *(if I'm shooting up this shit then I must be a drug addict!)*, which told me that maybe I didn't want to die after all. The crash was more terrifying too, and I could feel my kidneys, liver and brain swell up. No matter what method I used to get meth into my system, one thing that always felt the same was my body becoming a toxic-waste dumpsite.

Another thing: a tweeker was worthless and contemptible, not only to society at large but also in the eyes of every other drug addict. Heroin addicts pointed at methheads and said, "I may be fucked and strung out but that dude's a crazy disgusting asshole." It was true. There really was no such thing as a person who's not an asshole with meth in their bloodstream.

But the upside transcended all downers. Meth made the world orbit in a high-pitched hum of absolute exultation and nothing could touch you. Even when I was high as the sun I understood how meth was satisfying whatever need I had to destroy myself. Crystal meth would let you know that you're going out in a blaze of glory.

I got Serena's bag off a chair in the front room and handed it to her. She dug through it and pulled out that little plastic purse decorated with yellow and purple dancing bunnies. A dollar-store trinket designed to win smiles on little girls' faces. It made me sad. Felt like something innocent and intangible lost from childhood, a reminder of what was once possible before moms got lost and dads walked out forever.

She unzipped the purse and pulled from it a lighter and a glass pipe the color of dirty snow. Then she scraped some of the crushed meth off the Ramones CD into the bulbous end of the pipe, lifted it to her mouth, sparked the lighter and sucked. Then I took the pipe, scraped a good amount of the meth from the jewel case, lit it and sucked. The very idea of a lesser moment did not exist. I could hear variances in distortion off a gnat's wings across the room.

When I'd met Serena she was working fulltime at The Bush Cabin. Warehouse-sized and turd-colored, The Bush was designed to look like a giant log cabin. It didn't. It sat on a flat, treeless, six-lane highway in a fading industrial section on Phoenix's west side. A sun-scorched trailer park sat behind it and that's where Serena was holed up after she'd split up with this guy Mike. Mike ran a local beer distributor. He made good money and had kept Serena and her daughter on ice in a swanky condo inside a gated community where shiny SUVs filled parking spaces. She'd met Mike at The Bush. I saw him there once. Serena had pointed him out. He was your standard issue nude-bar regular, squat with creepy short fingers and steakhouse jowls, a guy who, in any other context, could never get a beautiful woman. She said she'd never fucked him, would only dance for him while he jerked off. As long as his balls were blue, she'd say, she'd get whatever she needed out of him. Yeah, that's what they all said. But I believed her.

The first thing Serena revealed to me was how beautiful her two-year-old daughter Cassidy was. The second thing she said was how her mother had just taken Cassidy away. Said the state would've if her mother hadn't. She told me how Mike had stormed into their place one evening accusing her of sucking a customer off at work, and then he punched her so hard that she hit her head and went out cold. The diaper-wearing Cassidy waddled out the front door and through the condo's parking lot. She somehow crawled under the perimeter fence and was nearly run over out on Bethany Home Road, a major Phoenix thoroughfare. A rush-hour driver managed to lift Cassidy to safety and get her up to the police station.

Then the cops responded to calls of a woman with a bruised eye hysterically screaming out along Bethany Home. Serena said her panic had only started to wane once the cops had her in custody. The cops, to their credit, reunited mom and daughter instead of arresting her. But they filed a report with Child Protective Services. Serena moved out of Mike's the following day but returned to meth for the first time since long before Cassidy was born.

One night Serena shared her history. She emerged from a long line of welfare recipients and molestation victims, and had never met her biological dad. Her grandmother, who everyone called Grams, pretty much raised Serena in San Bernardino trailer courts and biker bars. When Serena turned 12, her speed-freak uncle, a guy who raised back-alley gamecocks and dabbled in pit-bull barn fights, would sometimes shoot crystal into her and then into himself. Then he'd rape her.

Serena tilted her head back and blew meth from her lungs and I could see her heartbeat thumping in her neck at double Ramones speed. She refocused on the porn.

I sucked another bowl and was feeling great again when eager knuckles rapped the front door. No! Unannounced visitors were the bane of my existence, especially when I was spun out with porn and girl. Serena howled.

"Fuck." She killed the volume on the porn. "I was about to hit *it!*"

"Whoever's there knows we're home now, *thank you*," I said.

I tossed the pipe on the bed, slapped the towel around my waist, stumbled through the front room and swung the door open. A blast of obscene light hit my face. My pupils adjusted to a mud-colored United Parcel Service uniform. Sutter eyed me up and down like he always does, and pushed his lips together, the lower slightly protruding.

"Hey Julian, something from Hustler Video." He placed the box at my feet.

I never made eye contact with anyone when tweeked. Instead I tallied the concrete fissures on my tiny porch and noted dried sagebrush around his feet, and other dead, normally drought-tolerant desert plants needing to be swept away. Nothing lasts where it never rains.

"Awesome," I said.

Sutter delivered packages to my door twice weekly on

average. He was a deceptively youngish guy with dedicated facial lines, receding orange curls and blond eyebrows. My first impression months ago said pederast with an arrest record. The faint outline of a four-point Christian star extended about a quarter inch above and to the side of his brow ridge under his right eyebrow. A tweeker tattoo, to be sure, one a removal laser couldn't fully erase. I said to myself that no matter how fucked up I was I knew with absolute certainty that no tweek-on tat would ever decorate my brow, or anywhere on my body. I was also a judgmental piece of shit toward Sutter.

Because I knew but didn't want to believe that Sutter was looking at me but seeing himself, like I was seeing myself in his eyes. Compare and despair, as they say. Meth revealed the worst in everything, and then magnified it disproportionately. I'd X-ed out any capacity to see that Sutter's life might've unfurled in chancier, more challenging and enriching ways than my own. Meth cancels people around you.

The packages Sutter huffed to my door were from adult film production houses and the affixed labels were a dead giveaway — Big Tit Video, Private Media, Evil Angel, etc. The companies would send DVD porn titles for me to review. I reviewed porn for a living. Sutter understood the lethal mix of meth and sex and pornography. There's no duping another speed freak. He saw through all that external stuff — the dilated pupils and peeled-onion body stink, the stick-figure frame and cottonmouth non-sequiturs, and the perpetually spooked demeanor. It concealed the real stuff, the drawn-out weeks of dimensionless despair and self-hatred, the extended childhood dreams of escape that turned suicidal sometime during ninth grade, and the internal surrender that granted entrance to a self-obliterating never-never land.

The more porn he'd deliver to my door, the more I'd glean of his life too. How he'd lost a decade to the meth needle. Got addicted to hookers. He'd comb personal sex ads whenever he got high — "which was perfect," he'd say — because many of his girls were either addicted to meth or halfway there. During our brief conversations it became obvious that Sutter was offering himself as a sparkly example of clean, rehabbed existence.

He handed me the signature pad and poked his head inside my doorway, spying a place littered with empty 40-ounce beer bottles and piles of CDs, books, and porn DVDs.

I managed a jittery scrawl and followed his eyes through the living room, into the bedroom. He discovered Serena in her oily state of undress and he recoiled, embarrassed. I nudged him with the signature pad. He took it and withdrew his head from my space.

"I got a year clean," he said. "Did I already tell you that?"

"What?"

"That I feel amazing," he said. He did a quick little run in place, and added, "I even joined a gym."

"No shit?"

"And I didn't just hand my life over to god. Truth is, I found a dog."

Sweat stung my eyes. Sweating crank is like perspiring acid.

Sutter continued: "I found him half-dead, chained to an old fender behind my friend's place over near that Salvation Army on Van Buren. It was one hundred and ten degrees that day. If the little guy could withstand that, he's fairly close to some kinda god."

"I'll say," I said. I imagined Sutter nursing a little mangy dog back to health.

"You might've known the dog's owner," Sutter said.

"Everyone called him Rowdy. He swore that was his name. He's the only other white guy besides you that I ever saw living in this neighborhood."

I shook my head.

"He relapsed before his wife had left him. They found him last year out in the suburbs. Head caved in."

"*Jesus*," I said.

"Yeah. I still can't get over it. And you'd think, if anything, he'd have had his head caved in somewhere around here.

Sutter kept on about this dude Rowdy. It was strange because I was the spun out one and I couldn't even imagine Sutter jacked on crystal. I wanted him out of my face, but for some reason I couldn't just shut the door on him. I considered him a friend now. He seemed to give a shit. So, instead, with the towel clutched at my waist, I bent over and clumsily lifted the Hustler box with one arm and took a step back inside. I thought that'd signal him to split.

"I went to Rowdy's funeral and his ex-wife had showed up," he continued. "Shit. She brought along her ... " A flash of speed paranoia replaced his words: I was a dead dude in an unemployment line in room filled with incontinent boozers jackknifing on cots and I saw my own suicide, and then thought of my mother and felt sick to my stomach so I thought of Serena's uncle's molesting hands — those "big, soft and rude hands like a catcher's mitt with nails." Thought about how she split that scene at 15, fled to L.A., lied about her age, danced nude in Hollywood, and hung at the Rainbow and shitty motels with too many creeps, got greased on crystal meth and stayed awake for years. So much speeding and you'd never know it to just look at her. She was gorgeous.

Then I thought what a joke that I called myself a writer. I was a meth head.

I'd stay up three days straight and not eat. I'd rearrange a single sentence 60 or more times thinking each bettered the last but still wind up back where I started, the same words in exact succession. Then I'd move on to the next line. Two sentences could take hours and they sucked, just half-baked ideas propped up on adjective support. For timeouts I'd engage in long hours of porno jerk sessions, pissing into empty beer bottles so as not to get up and interrupt the action. Pretty soon I merely existed, not "being" nor "doing." The very definition of the living dead.

I remembered this one night I was sitting at the computer writing up a review of a porn movie. I hadn't eaten for two days, had downed gallons of beer. By then I'd watched hours and hours of spurious cuckolds and staged glory holes and prolapsed rectums and was coughing up bad Lester Bangs run-ons about it all and it'd been hours since finishing the last of my crank and I wanted to die because my head and body screamed and nothing less than meth would fix things. You can only imagine how deadline panic can exacerbate need for crystal. So I ended up inside a murky house with tin-foiled windows inhabited by a trio of tweeked crystal dealers who bred fighting pit bulls. The place reeked of armpits and dog shit and prison. Baying dogs in the back sounded like coyotes ripping apart children. Right in the kitchen one scabbed-up champ with dead eyes and a sculpted torso was neck-strapped to some kind of treadmill, sprinting straight at nowhere. Either the treadmill stopped or his heart did.

A vampire in the sun had nothing on me, all sick-edgy in the doorway, heartbeat jackhammering visibly on my chest, a fucked-up earnest angel with tweek-on tattoos rabbiting on in my face. I had to get back inside and close the door. He was keeping me in that horrible sunlit doorway on purpose, just to fuck with me.

I blurted something and my tongue stuck to the roof of my mouth. Gibberish. Again, but slower: "Dude. *I need to go.*" Sutter finally shut up.

He said, "Oh, shit. Sorry, man."

He stepped from the porch, but before I had the door closed, he stopped and looked back. "You know, some guy said something the other night that made a hell of a lot of sense. He said 'If you find yourself in a hole, just stop digging.'"

I nodded. "We sure can count on living to make life a shit-ton harder, huh?" I said.

I carried the parcel inside and kicked the door closed behind me. It's amazing how much better you feel when you're tweeking and you step back into your privacy, away from sobriety. I quickly pulled a dirty knife from the kitchen sink, placed the box on the chair and cut it open. Like every other box I received from the porno companies, this contained advance copies of factory-packaged DVDs cushioned in packing peanuts, plastic bubble wrap and a shipping invoice with "No Charge" typed in the payments received box. There was brand-newness inside these boxes that Sutter hauled to my door — the only freshness in a life that had stalled out on downed hopes. I reached in, pulled out the stack of DVDs and sifted through the titles, all of which were silly: *Butt Worship Vol. 47, Chicks Peggin' Boys, Lesbo Soul Sisters and so on …*

Most studios included photocopied pictures of porn actresses holding IDs next to their faces, for legal reasons, to prove that the girls were of age so venders and magazines and websites had proof that they were not trafficking child porn. The IDs gave away the real names and addresses of the actresses. Real smart. Many girls used check-cashing IDs to show who they were, which only deepened a creeping sense of sadness in the images. The grained faces, fleshless and without expression, foundation makeup barely covering troubled complexions, hinted that there were no soothing words that could've been uttered by any mother to reconcile bleak consequences in their early teens.

The pictures were the flipside to male-defined slut images in ass shorts and hooker boots. Most pictured wore street clothes that suggested rural Christian Americana more than anything hipster or hooker: baggy blue jeans and hearts on delicate chains, not Suicide Girl sexual self-awareness in body ink and cheeky winks. They looked lost to something bigger, visions of money and celebrity, and easily persuaded from one unhappy place to another unhappy place with yet more compromises.

My Catholic upbringing ensured sex stayed dirty. But your head had to be inverted on meth to enjoy these lost souls and their drippy, grinding anatomies. One cruel consequence to so much meth is that despite hours and days of hyper-focused anatomical fetishizing and wholly insatiable sexual quirks, your dick doesn't work.

I carried the box into the bedroom. Serena was sitting upright in bed, on the thinning side of zaftig, glistening tan lines, raven bob. The four Ramones covered in bitter talcum.

She looked up, eyebrows lifting above dilated sky-blue saucers, and said, "Really? More porn? Jesus."

Moans rose from the tiny TV speaker: a submissive couple devoted to a mistress specializing in suffocation. *Oh, God. Jesus, I can't breath …*

I felt it stir inside, and moved.

Hell descended on the 72-hour slam of meth and sex and porn. No way back up, no easy way down and no choices. I my future and past had darkened into repulsive shapes that unfurled repetitively like Japanese horror movies. Godless yearnings. Anatomical warfare. Loud Ramones guitars and high-pitched hisses of a million cicadas going at it, and fading in and out. In and out.

The sun rose and dropped, rose and dropped again. And soon all that was left was excruciating need to scale the internal electric fences, where out beyond the front door a stupidly innocent moon glowed like some hole that god carved out of black.

Grams

Grams

I

Sprock was once an All Everything star in high-school
football and now he's the doorman. He was a real
beast of a doorman too. It was like his outsized sports
ambition had been reeled in and stuffed inside his suit. The
sleeves and legs came up short and the jacket bunched up where
his arms stuck out. His house-like shoulders made his head
look freakily small. I figured the employee dress code must've
heightened whatever sense of resentment and humiliation that
rose inside of him after he blew his knee out playing college ball
over at Arizona State. There was desperation, and that made
him appear mean. But he wasn't mean at all. Just cornered, and
he was compensating for it. For example, each of his fingers
sported gold and diamond rings and he had a scary wraparound
neck tattoo that rose above his collar and up his chin, showing
a trio of fang-heavy rattlesnakes spelling out the words
GRIDIRON FOR LIFE.

His mostly idle exercise of authority was solid enough to
demonstrate that he was indeed the keeper of civility here, that
drunken construction crews and frat-house bros would never

challenge him, nor would they lay a hand on any of the dancers, so great was his presence.

Then one night I watched him let it all out on some Mötley Crüe leftover. I'd seen this guy around. He was hooked up with one of the dancers, and forever tedious in a uniform of motorcycle boots, wallet chain, and sleeve tats. He was apparently blind to the fact it'd been more than a decade since Nirvana exterminated his kind. He'd since retreated to the dark recesses of west Phoenix with his girl and was always at the club whenever she was working. She supported him and still believed he'd one day be a rock star. He had a shitty complexion and sloppy drunken energy and one of those tick-tock tempers that masqueraded arrogantly as confidence and at any moment could erupt. He always seemed eager to fight. It was a comportment that must've been tested all his life, one that ballooned into a psychosis once he started adding crystal meth to his steady diet of Jack. I'd heard he was a jealous prick who controlled every aspect of his girlfriend's life.

Sprock was just waiting for this guy to unload on his girlfriend in public. And that night he finally did.

The Crüe dude resembled a ragdoll as Sprock tossed him around the lighted parking lot. His head made a loud, echoing thud as it bounced off the sleek finish of some customer's sparkly SUV. His burgundy-haired girlfriend could only watch from the entrance, mostly with head down and one hand shielding her face. She had one purple-y eye and runny mascara, and wore a pink shawl over a g-string and white go-go-boots.

When the fracas ended, that is, when Sprock had had enough, he pushed the guy loose, saying, "consider yourself banned for life." Crüe dude's wifebeater was torn and bloody, as was his face; his nose ring had been torn out and his head bandana was lost to the wind. He was half-looking for both as he stumbled around the parking lot, blustered and hoarsely shouting shit at his girlfriend. The commotion continued until Crüe dude found his bandana, slid it over his burgundy-highlighted blue-black mop and begin stumbling, bloody face and all, straight up Grand Avenue, backlit by cars and semi-trailer trucks whizzing by. After a good 50 yards he spun around to face us and, while walking backwards, shouted, with his fists jacking the air, "Fuck you, *bitches*." Then he turned and continued on, punching imaginary faces in front and above him. I watched him disappear into the night. Somehow I felt sorry for him.

Sprock returned to his post at the door. I stepped over the velvet rope that arched on brass columns along the sidewalk, a couple of feet from the entrance. He nodded me into the club, which saved me the eight-buck door charge.

All-nude bars required a cover because they can't sell alcohol, because Arizona law stated that booze and glistening female anatomy in bars don't mix. One thing they got right. But The Bush Cabin got your money — and skirted the law. The 21-and-over club was split in two. There was a "topless" side, where you could go and get hammered, and the other "totally nude" side (or "totaly nude" per the hand-painted sign in the parking lot) where they only sold soft drinks. You could get drunk on the topless side and then wander over to the nude side. But you had to pay a cover either way. Smart.

Sprock's nod-through was generous, not only because I was broke but also because it allowed me a bogus, fuck-yeah-I'm-a-somebody-asshole sensation that'd last until I'd leave. Whatever class system existed inside The Bush, I was in an elevated one, opposite that of the world outside.

See, the DJs often spun a Spent Saints song call "Keep it Tall" for the dancers, one that made no sense in a playlist crammed with insipid rap and shitty metal. You have no idea what it does to watch a woman lithely spread, purl and tease, for cash, to a song you holed up in some room for hours to create, in this case, and in my mind at least, a misunderstood singsong of undying existential collapse in the guise of keeping it hard, man.

That helped because I'd been hollowed out for months, indifferent to anything, and the magic of drinking had stopped working. I was too dulled to think through ideas, much less take action on them. Physical movement was an unconscious collection of weary processes. Great songs, books and movies no longer held sway. Curiosities in small wonders died. So, yeah, getting waved through a grim entrance of a west Phoenix nude bar lifted me up. It'd come down to that.

A giant grizzly in the foyer greeted all. Dead with outstretched arms, jagged teeth and glassy eyes, he was 12-feet-tall and six-feet wide and looked as if he'd been starving at the time of his death.

The Bush's interior was like heaven's rec room for nature-hating suburban beer-swills who'd succumbed to their own internal dissolutions — Bud Light flapper ads, sports on flatscreens, stunned taxidermy on fake wood grain, a nude dancer working the pole.

The stage's elevated, woodsy bling repeated in strategically placed mirrors, extravagance thin and propped up as a cash-strapped movie set. Whole scene stank of jasmine and Jäger and vanilla, and the low-end from Crüe and Pantera kicked my heart into off-sync fibrillations. It was ritualistic as all get out.

As I entered, a rockabilly-tinged dancer in red cowboy boots was finishing her set. I went and relaxed against a pole a good six feet from the stage, which was perfectly round and lighted in the colors of Gummi Bears candy.

A handful of dancers sat alone at various places around the room, chatting up a few customers, bored in g-strings. Long hair, short hair, zaftig, spindly, crank-addled or straight, some old, some young, most too sad.

A DJ piped in over the sound system as the last song faded out on rockabilly girl, a voice low and insincere. "Gentlemen, up next is the exotic and sultry Ramona! Please put your hands together for the sexy …" Marilyn Manson's Gary Glitter-fettered "The Dope Show" erupted from the strip bar's sound system and quick bursts of fog created a cloud at the back of the stage. She emerged through it, sinuous in tats and piercings, and a vulgar ballet ensued.

She was wearing a sheer babydoll and black spiked knee-highs, and stage lights revolved above her like flittering orchids, taking in her curves, upholding her pouty theater. It was half-designed to extract money from clammy palms of the drunk and the dead, half-designed to make the night livable. A masterclass in sexualized make-believe of what men want.

An ill-defined yearning eased over me and I pretended that I really had made something of myself, that the days ahead weren't just drunken fanfares to hasten the grave. A dream granting me entrance into a peaceful world of happy amnesia.

Keeping with the deliberate sway of hips and the song's annoyingly synthetic glam beat, Ramona slipped the babydoll up over her head and slung it aside. Nude but for boots, she slid down the pole and then up and slowly bent all the way over, lipping Manson's lyrics, her black, blunt-backed hair dusting the lighted stage floor, she peered between her legs upside-down, offering full view of her ass for those on barstools. Pretty sure she was tallying bald spots in the angled mirrors above the bar. It wasn't yet 9 p.m., still early on a Friday. No money. She half turned and lifted her head and arched her back, out-stretching her arms like wings, distending the butterfly tattoo between her natural breasts, and studied her movements in the floor-to-ceiling mirrors in front of her.

She straightened up, rested her head against the pole, and dropped down about two feet, extending her legs out in a V shape. Her hands slipped slowly over her breasts and down between her legs, self-adoration begat a delicately faked climax; trembling, eyes closed. Then she was up along the edge of the stage, lithesome and formative, and slightly behind the beat. I was dumbstruck into a kind of melancholy that can't simply be explained away; it's visceral, unremitting, fueled on longing. One of three bored men sitting down on floor chairs stood and dropped a single dollar tip on the stage. They weren't seeing it. They weren't seeing her. How can that be?

Ramona was up and centered on the perfectly round stage, as the song waned. She spun on her heel, and with her back arched, she eased forward and snatched the dollar from the stage with her lips. Then she was done like an invisible curtain had dropped. Ramona collected her costume and sashayed from the stage with that confidence.

Her song faded into Guns N' Roses "Sweet Child O' Mine" as the DJ introduced Susie Sioux, "a comely squaw imported all the way from Superior, Arizona." In a minute Ramona was standing before me, smelling of vanilla and sweat, wearing a purple g-string and that sheer babydoll.

"Buy me something to drink?" she said without blinking. That's how I met Ramona. Her real name was Serena.

II

I remember that first time I did meth. Before that I was perfectly happy just drinking, mostly beer. Beer was easy, and legal. I'd been hooked up with Serena for a few months. She was high on something and I couldn't figure out what. At first I thought it was just weed, her normal constant, but it was something else entirely.

It didn't register that I was with a methhead; I thought those freaky monomanias were wired into her DNA. Beyond the chronic sleeplessness and incessant cleaning of her tiny trailer — which was crammed with Ramones posters and swag — there were her uncanny skills on the stripper stages, which more and more I saw betrayed a sexual and personal disconnect. She was doing what she thought she had to do to survive. She hid it well but it was making her crazy.

Then she'd stayed up for three nights straight, and was going into her fourth, when her depleted system had finally yielded to a few hours of sleep. That's when I explored her purse. I wanted to get high too. I was searching for anything when I found little yellow scabs of meth inside a tiny baggie stuffed inside a plastic coin purse.

I slipped into the bathroom and dumped a rock onto a hand-held mirror. It looked like a piss-yellow tooth with specks and spots of black, like decay. It stunk like armpits and toilet cleaner when I flattened it into a little pancake of damp talcum. I used a painter's blade to etch out three thick, two-inch lines, like cocaine. I carefully rolled up the one-dollar bill I had. I snorted a line and there was fire, like somebody had flicked a lighter flame into my nostril. A second later it torched my brain. Soon the heart rate doubled, spiked inside my temples, and the night crystallized. Armed battalions marched into my nervous system and obliterated the cognitive roadblocks to all avenues of happiness erected over the years. Millions of endorphins were set free.

So good was meth I didn't need booze. Hand a suicidal alcoholic a concoction whose rush is an express train away from the tattooed herds, the tract-house grids, the dollar-store depression and an entire whole world designed for the well-adjusted, and I'll show you an instant drug addict, no booze necessary. I'd play my guitar and two brand new songs would come complete. Kitchen cleaned. The bathroom, tub and basin too. Weeds pulled. World anew.

Sure, I was a bastard to rifle through her purse and steal her shit. I'm sure she counted on it to erase the crash and ten-hour horror that was cosmetology school. Given her state, such as it was, she needed it. Guilt panged me throughout the entire next day. But that drug. Jesus. It's no wonder a whole class of hurting humans instantly get strung out on it.

I knew Serena was waging other inner battles. I never met her daughter Cassidy, but I understood how her daughter was a quiet source of Serena's agony — that is, she wasn't a mother to her, not when I knew her. That fact got me down. I wanted her to be a mother to Cassidy. Why couldn't she (us) just be OK and normal? But she was all messed up on crystal.

She'd lost herself and was scared, kind of like how I'd lost myself and was scared. We had that, and pheromones and meth. Neither of us could begin to articulate or define ourselves in any way that had meaning, and we too-often communicated in cotton-mouthed dirges, the parlance of the wasted and the numb. Crystal made sure she was blind to her options and possibilities, which were hard for her to see anyway. I'd met her at her worst. I was taking advantage of a kind and beautiful woman who was skidding out. She never asked me for anything, and there was nothing I could give her anyway. She deserved better than me.

Some nights I'd pass out drunk and come to at sunrise and she'd be wide-awake and sweaty beside me. Her eyes fixed on the Ramones' black-and-white Presidential seal logo, a silky tapestry tacked up above the bed. I'd peer up from the bed and focus on that logo and listen to the rattling room fan and the distant 18-wheelers shifting gears out on Grand Avenue, and every once in awhile the sad train whistle from a Union Pacific freight line making its way down to Tucson. Sometimes I'd hear Serena cry, softly. She wanted her daughter back.

She'd fight for hours to stay motionless in bed, for me, feigning rest and sleep while her heart pounded away and her head buzzed like fluorescent lights. Imagine eight hours of that, compounded by hallucinations borne of a weeklong meth grind. Once she told me of "wicked and scaly serpents" who'd reached into her bedroom window and lifted her to the skies and whispered to her throughout the night that everything would be OK.

Within weeks after that first snort I was scoring crystal off the popsicle man. Crank and a couple Lick-a-Color Ice Bars. He was a Latino kid who'd christened himself Dylan when he crossed over to Arizona after leaving his Culiacán, Mexico home. He said he first learned English by listening to his dad sing Bob Dylan songs phonetically. He drove this nipple-pink ice cream truck nearly every afternoon. Cartoony ice-cube letters spelled out "Soft Tastee" on its sides and back, and a loud and distorted version of "Pop Goes the Weasel" looped through a speaker attached to the roof. On days when I had money I'd hear that horrible song rise from blocks away and I'd rush out the door, just like I did as a kid.

Scoring drugs this way was kid-tested safe. Exchanges were cheerful and Dylan knew what I wanted. I'd slip him bills and he'd slip the baggie of meth between Lick-a-Colors. But there were downsides. For starters, you were participating in a trade that was leaving absolute human wreckage in its wake. And you don't know guilt until you're standing at that side-door hatch purchasing drugs alongside a handful of happy Mexican kids, sometimes standing with their moms and dads.

Dylan's crystal wasn't the dirty yellow hillbilly shit with the black specs in it; this was purer, clear as fogged glass and hard like rice, from Mexico. I learned it was best to score from the Mexicans because they were a lot more honest, from good Catholic families headed by strong matriarchs.

I'd try never to buy from rednecks and hillbillies. Nine times out of ten they were emotionally damaged, oily headed folk spun on their own crank and bat-shit crazy, which made them paranoid, and, therefore, armed. They wouldn't hesitate to make you wait in their squalid places and jones for your jack and test your patience with their insane existences. It wasn't the sticky kids with Down Syndrome in dirty diapers amidst the porn, the guns, and the beer that sickened the most, nor was their talk of wanting to fuck your girlfriend's ass. They'd say so in front of her. How they might want to fuck your ass too. Nah. What frightened was the madness embedded deep inside their eyes. I learned to tread lightly so as to not suddenly have a pistol pressed to my skull.

If I had no money I'd phone up my pal Tinkles, who always knew where to go, and he'd front it to me if he had to. But I'd have to wait for him, sometimes 10 or 12 hours. Tinkles had a job. He'd been employed in fast food for what seemed like forever, even worked his way up to franchise manager of a Burger King. He was the only employed speed freak I knew. He was a close friend who understood, without discussion, moral compasses gone completely haywire.

III

Jump forward some months. Serena and I were preparing to leave my place. We'd been up for a few days. Showered, dressed, shaky, malnourished, dehydrated, depressed, and wearing sunglasses, we smeared gobs of super-sunblocker skin protection on exposed areas. It stung to touch my skin. We were ready for the three-mile trek north to Grams' apartment. Grams is Serena's grandmother, and because neither of us had a car —and we were out of cash and crank, and well into the all-consuming ache of a meth famine, we had to walk to borrow her car so we could drive to the west side to score from a dealer who traded meth for porn. Serena had called him that morning before the sun came up. He said he'd be home.

Before we split, I selected from towering stacks a few dozen newly released porn titles and dropped them into a grocery bag. Months ago I discovered that the promo porn DVDs the companies sent me to review for adult magazines doubled as "meth vouchers" because some meth dealers would trade gobs of crystal for top-studio porn titles, particularly those not yet on store shelves. Porn's the cross addiction's chokehold for a methhead, way more so than booze, or any other drug — it fires the brain's pleasure receptors into insane, days-long sexual overdrives. So the DVDs were as good as grams of crystal, especially to Red Colt, a dealer Serena introduced me to at The Bush.

We stepped outside, and I closed the door behind us. The sun was agony, blinding.

In the dirt courtyard outside my place, under an arch of mesquite and Palo Verde tree branches, a crippled sparrow hopped in frenzied circles, one wing flapping in the dirt attempting to fly. Thinking I could somehow nurse her back to health, I bent down to catch her but she scurried away terrified and disappeared under the trees.

Serena watched the bird and adjusted her sunglasses. She looked great in super-tight black stretch jeans, high-top Converse All-Stars and an old Stones *Some Girls* T-shirt that once belonged to her dad. "I don't think I can make it to Grams's," she said. "The heat, man … I feel like I'm going to die."

"You'll be fine, baby," I said, knowing too well the hellish walk ahead. "We'll be there and then we'll score and then we'll be in heaven."

"We need to fucking quit this shit …"

"I know," I said. "I know."

We stuck to shaded areas on side streets. Every dude in every car, and some women, stared at Serena's ass. It only heightened the humiliation of our walk. And the sun: when hatred burns down like that, and you're on a meth crash, the unacceptable can become acceptable and insane logic can rule. The other day a random motorist blew away a total stranger who was driving the car beside his. This shooter didn't use one of those Arizona-legal concealed weapons and merely pull the trigger because the other guy had yelled some shit. Folks in these parts have been known to do that and avoid jail time, which is incredible if you think about it. Nah, this guy pulled an M11 machine gun and sprayed the other guy's head into the far lane, decorating both a storefront window and some poor woman on the bus-stop bench. That's some meth action for sure, down here in the valley of the spun.

Jittery and sweating foul tweeker poisons, we made it to a Circle K and counted out quarters for coffee. Coffee's the classic methhead tonic when drugs run out because it slows the crash and provides a minor reactivation that can get you through unconscionable moments. The hot caffeine tricks you into believing you've done more speed, and you actually feel slightly happy again for a minute or three. I've drunk gallons of hot Circle K coffee in the middle of summertime, lord knows. You can always spot a tweeker at a Circle K too. They'll be counting out coins for coffee under tomb-raised hairstyles, bones and eyes rattling inside scabbards, and they'll split on a shitty ill-fitting bike, or on foot. There was no way to hide the truth in public.

IV

We arrived at Serena's grandmother's place and the sun was well into the sky. She lived in one of those drab, L-shaped, two-story apartment complexes in central Phoenix that looked like a Best Western motel in 1971. It had a watered, neatly trimmed lawn under tall, symmetrically arranged palm trees and a book-shaped swimming pool in the courtyard.

Grams swung the door open after what felt like a thousand knocks. I saw a frail, hunch-backed old thing with a ghoulish grin and a mess of unwashed snow-white hair. Serena threw her arms up in mock frustration, said, "Finally, Grams. Jeeze!"

Grams, jutting her bony, muumuu'd hip to one side, said in mock southern-privilege sorority, "I had lady business in the bathroom."

Serena smiled, stepped forward and squeezed her tight. Grams' face rested on Serena's shoulder and when she saw me her grin vanished. I read her mind: Another tit-bar loser getting into her granddaughter's pants, spending every bit of her tit-bar money. A TV voice from inside her apartment boomed on about motorized stair-climbers.

Her one-bedroom place was shadowy, dusty, depressing. Felt like four p.m. all day long in there, and smelled of Pine-Sol and instant mashed potatoes. Nothing in her apartment ever fully came into focus. It looked as though someone filled it with sticky Easter trappings and Native American textiles gave it a good, snow-globe shake and then set it back down again.

But the angels. Serena forewarned of Grams' quirks — namely, a predilection for daisy-print muumuus, tabloid TV and these armies of ceramic shelf angels, the disturbing kind found in dollar stores and on late-night infomercials. Her angels populated about every flat surface in her apartment, including the kitchen and bathroom. They were arranged on the floor in long rows, leaving enough space for movement in front of the TV and around the couch, and a narrow pathway to both the bathroom and bedroom. Glow-in-the-dark cherubs dangled randomly from gilded Christmas tree garlands that arched between curtain rods. Grams came unglued, Serena warned, if an angel was touched in any way.

Serena neglected to add that Grams favored a pail of water and washcloth over a shower and bath, and would sometimes spontaneously bust out the suds on the kitchen floor in front of visitors.

We came inside and sat down on the couch. "I've got lemon cake," Grams said, stepping into the kitchen. Serena spoke into her cell phone, hung up and gave me that all-will-be-well look.

Then she whispered that Red wasn't fond of entertaining more than one buyer at a time. Of course he wasn't. He wanted to fuck Serena.

"Just stay with Grams," Serena said.

Grams came back and handed us each a slice of lemon cake on a paper plate with a plastic fork. It was stale and dry. I took one bite, forced it down into my cotton mouth and set the plate on the coffee table.

Serena got up and went to the kitchen sink. She grabbed a tall glass, filled it and drank it. Then she filled it again and brought it to me and I downed it in one long pull. I placed the glass on the coffee table next to the piece of lemon cake. Serena sat back down and announced to Grams that she needed to borrow her car because she had an errand to run. She forced down some cake, which wasn't easy for her either, then stood up, collected the grocery bag with the porn, Grams' car keys, and wrapped a hand around the doorknob and began to turn it when Grams looked at me and said, "You ain't goin' with her?"

Serena stopped, looked back at her and said, as if I wasn't there, "No, Grams. Julian doesn't need to stand in line with me to renew my driver's license."

"Then where the hell is his damn car?"

"Oh, Grams. He don't bite!"

"You're going to have to put gas in it!" Grams said.

The door closed and I listened to Serena's footsteps disappear. I felt Grams' glare on the side of my face while I untangled in my mind the two copulating monkeys in a field of pastel flowers in a framed scene on the wall.

"He don't talk much neither, does he?" she said to no one.

V

Grams settled into her chair, and, after a tense moment fumbling with her TV remote, tuned into an obvious daytime favorite, a talk show hosted by a silver-headed guy who's adored by grandmothers easily wooed by celebrity when it appears on TV in dark Armani. What I saw was a media chicken-hawk weaned in local-TV journalism who seized the addictive powers of the breakdown of American civilization and bottled it up for mass consumption five days a week. The money. The ass. The dream.

The crank jones killed any potential for comfort. As if to hurry Serena's return, I invented a tracking meter in my head that updated her movements in real time: She promised Grams to put gas in her car. That meant she'll put our last three bucks in at Indian School and 7th Avenue. Should take about six minutes. Drive west to Red's cinderblock shithole near Glendale and 15th Avenue. Should take about 12 minutes one way in weekday traffic. That's 18 minutes so far. A snag: Serena must barter the porn DVDs for speed. Shit. That'll eat more time. Red'll lobby to watch some porn with her as part of the exchange. Aw, fuck.

Our eyes fixed on the TV. An exasperated mother learned that her 18-year-old daughter was doing "punk rock" porn. The girl must be punk rock because she wore a flimsy wifebeater patched with an anarchy star, it's lower half torn off just below her nipples. Her basement-white skin was a canvas of predictable tats; fake prison spider webs, a shamrock with a 666, and a Misfits skull that ran elbow to shoulder, and piercings. Black hot pants, thigh-high stockings and dirty-red Converse completed the visual absurdity.

Maybe Red wouldn't be spun out. Maybe he wouldn't be turning routine chores into insurmountable complications, like most tweekers I'd met. I once suffered an agonizing wait for speed while Red transformed a simple oil change for his pickup truck into an overhaul of its driveshaft, right there in his dirt-weed front yard. His greasy, shirtless drama needed an audience. Must've been 115 degrees in the shade that day.

And maybe he'd save his illiterate, long-winded Aryan Brotherhood horseshit for his tweeker buds, those west side hillbillies who stomped about in red-laced Doc Martens with girlfriends who never uttered a word.

Grams didn't overlook the porn star's diastematic smile and run-on sentences. I figured the girl probably reminded her of Serena. She sneered, "Disgusts me to no end." Then the TV mother confronted the daughter and tragic gold ensued. Mom pleaded, daughter laughed, and Grams shook her head.

But Serena's need was my need too and she'd never oblige an asshole racist whose sunken, sickness-streaked eyes rarely strayed from her hips and ass. She'd learned to handle much bigger douchebags in the strip bars. She'd yield to the drug joneses to a point and oblige the fucker a bit of dirty talk, he might have to peel one off while she danced, and then …

A commercial break. Grams stood up and stepped among angels to the kitchen, lifted a plastic bucket from beneath the sink, filled it with hot water and placed it in the center of the kitchen floor. She then walked back to collect a washcloth from the pantry and a bar of soap from the bathroom. The TV squawked on. She returned to the bucket and hastily removed her muumuu and underwear. Grams' skin hung from her bones like liquefied taffy. It had the color of contusions, peppered by areas of liver gray. An ash-toned tat of a black winged angel rose from flames, stretched from her navel to clavicle, and grazed the inner sides of her sagging breasts, and drooped like a 50-year-old racial slur.

My need turned inward. I dreamed of weird shit, like slicing one of my eyeballs open to let the panic escape and then taking a horse-sized hypodermic filled with pure dopamine and shooting it into my skull.

OK, a guess said 20 minutes at Red's. She'd shave three minutes off the return trip because when speed's in hand, lookout. Countdown clock, go baby, go. …

Grams placed her feet on either side of the bucket, squatted as if peeing outdoors, and began to clean her upper body with the soap and washcloth. The porno star kid enlightened mom of HIV screenings and multiple partners and Grams washed, stretching skin up into wrinkled curls that left red streaks. The TV mom's voice lifted. She didn't raise her little girl to be no whore, and Grams worked the suds and cloth with more force. TV girl crowed about how her star rose on bukkake showers and father-daughter fetishes, and Grams pulled her dripping hands down, down over the angel, and pressed the soap and washcloth between her legs and, in long strokes, scrubbed front to back, back to front. Porn mom's shoulders dropped in resignation. The daughter continued; her voice descended into a godless drone of anal sex and multiple insertions. The audience gasped. Grams stood, lips tight, eyes squeezed shut, head bouncing side to side. Her arms lifted and flailed like a terror-stricken beekeeper, sending water and suds raining down in the kitchen, down on all the angels.

VI

I used Grams' landline to call Serena on her cell. Hours had passed. I tried Serena again. Again and again. I don't want to even think about how many times I used Grams' phone to call her. Straight to voicemail. Motherfucker.

Darkness crammed windows, and the only light that shone upon Grams was from the TV, full of face-lifted preeners. The same light gave edges to the countless angels that marched back into dark recesses of that apartment. Beer would ease the pain. I only had nickels in my pocket and Grams kept no alcohol in her place. Serena hadn't returned. I was about to down the mouthwash in the bathroom.

Grams said, finally, "So Serena left you here with me?"

I didn't say anything.

"It isn't the first time she's pulled a stunt like this," she added.

I stayed quiet. Then she laughed. But there was no joke. Why did she have to laugh? She turned to face to me, and she said, in a creepy little-girl voice, "peep-peep, pop-pop."

Had no idea what that meant.

I finally phoned my pal Tinkles. He collected me after he finished his shift at Burger King. He brought beer, Southern Comfort and some bitter yellow-y meth, which did the trick. He dropped me off at home and left me with a little bit of that speed and beer. Dear god, Tinkles was a real live angel.

I finished the speed and beer and stayed up all night again, but still worried sick and panicked about Serena. Speed usually fixes that shit, initially. Serena never showed up at Grams'.

After some frantic phone calling I discovered that Serena ran into an old girlfriend, a white stripper who called herself Cheyenne, at the dealer's place. They got high and decided they'd move to Las Vegas that night. That's how crystal sometimes works. You do things like move to Vegas the very night you think of it, leaving behind and in the dark those who might give a shit about you. They loaded Cheyenne's 1995 T-top Trans Am and split. Their plan was to find legit dancing work in casino party pits.

I spent the next morning pacing and crashing and hurting. Serena never did return any of my calls.

Finally "Pop Goes the Weasel" rose in the distance, echoing in the streets, moving closer.

I went outside, crossed the courtyard, and stood under the trees to wait. A dozen or so Mexican girls were gathering in the chain-linked front yard across the street. Faces filled with light and wonder reflected in carefully considered attires, shoes polished black, white anklets. Some had flowers in their hair. One girl wore a magenta *quinceañera* dress with waist bows and lace sleeves. Proud parents with cameras hovered around them. Catholic guilt rose like upchuck; meth and the sacrament of the Eucharist and the penance.

Then Dylan and his popsicle truck and "Pop Goes the Weasel" rounded the corner, rattled up the street. I stepped out, he saw me and stopped. He was wearing a cowboy hat. It was the first time I'd ever seen him in one. It was white and it gave him a bigger presence, more in control. He looked at my face. He knew. I went to the passenger side door and he rolled the window down. Using all I had to not appear desperate — which likely only heightened the outward appearance of my own desperation, as is common with any scummy drug addict — I said, shakily, "Compadre, man. Could you hook me up? Only thing is, I'll have to pay you later."

A look of concern dropped over his face and he shook his head slowly. He contemplated for a second and looked up the street. Then he nodded tentatively.

"OK," he said. No smile this time.

Wow. I wouldn't front this shit to anyone.

He reached into the top pocket of his cowboy shirt and pulled out a little baggie and handed it to me. I carefully pushed the gram into my pants pocket. The knotted anxiety in my gut yielded to elation.

"Thank-you-thank-you-thank-you," I said, adding, "I'll have the money in two days," which was a lie. I had no dollars coming in. No gigs lined up. I hated to lie to him. But he knew. It was obvious, which made me feel worse. I stepped away, he motored up the street and "Pop Goes the Weasel" kicked in. I looked to the girls across the street. I wondered why they didn't run to the ice cream truck. Instead they'd formed a line, hands joined like a string of cutout dolls. All smiles. I turned back, away. I moved through the arch of conjoining mesquite and Palo Verde trees into the shade, out of that pitiless sun and into darkness.

Serena did finally call me, weeks later. She was back dancing nude, working the peepshows. She wanted her life back, and her daughter Cassidy. She cried. That day at Grams' apartment was the last I ever saw her.

The Old Ladies in Church Hats

The Old Ladies in Church Hats

I was driving home after a party one night with my right hand covering my right eye while the left held the steering wheel and attempted to keep the car on the road. It wasn't easy to keep that piece-of-shit Ford Escort from bouncing off curbs. It was February and the roads were icy and the tires were bald. This wasn't the West and I never learned how to drive wretched roads streaked in ice and snow. We must've hit the curb at least a half-dozen times along Woodward Avenue after it narrowed into downtown, and after heading the wrong-way on one-way streets doubly obscured by the snow and that steam that spews from Detroit's manhole covers, on our way to Beaubien Street, where we lived.

Riding shotgun was my girlfriend Jenna, who was mostly passed out. She was in a foul mood too and had that grudging jaw. When I swerved to avoid what I thought was a duck and slammed into a giant pothole, which was momentarily sobering enough to realize there was no duck wandering across the below-freezing Detroit street, Jenna's head bounced hard against the passenger's side window. That got her going about my shitty driving. Then she went off on the blue hairs stepping from the garish Greektown Casino into idling shuttle busses at 2 a.m., armed with shoulder-bag oxygen tanks. At this hour the buses and the casino's pulsing arteries of gold and its phallic neon sign provided the only lights in downtown Detroit, lights that delivered those old folks to places far from the city's wreckage. That they are even here at this hour in the morning was always a wonder.

We made it home. No matter how drunk we were on any given night, or whose eye was negotiating the actual roadways, no matter where we were in Detroit, we'd always managed to pull that dented Escort into that ugly, dark, pot-holed parking lot and stumble into our building. It was miraculous. Of course, it never hurt our chances that Detroit traffic laws were optional—city cops had better things to do than surveil city streets for drunk drivers. After closing time on any given night you'll see rusted-out jalopies and silver SUVs and aging pimp Caddies all swerving on the streets like herrings fighting upstream. A drunkard's paradise.

I should've been dead though. Death was an entertainable option for me because I wasn't grateful for being alive. That made me a real gentleman. I stopped giving a shit in a city that didn't give a shit. Detroit can do that to you the same way the booze can do that to you. An old meth dealer back in Arizona, this guy called Jesus, once told me during one of my five-day speed benders that if you don't give a shit about living you're pretty much invincible.

My general attitude toward life directly reflected the city of Detroit, which is a ruin, really. All jagged edges and cold hard lines and darkness. It's the most god-forsaken failure of a once-great American industrial giant that you could ever dream up. In spring and summer and fall you can actually taste the city's desolation. The wind carries particles of wood and rust from husks of abandoned houses and crumbling auto factories, so you're actually breathing into your lungs the city of Detroit, and sometimes coughing it up. It gets into your blood that way, your nervous system. That sense of diminished achievement and failure gets inside of you, and mostly when you're unaware. So you move around the city with this oppression in your system, and it floats all around you too because anywhere you look in Detroit you see decay – in its population, in its infrastructure, in its quality of life. After a while you sputter and stop like a car after someone dumped salt into its gas tank.

In wintertime things get smaller, insular. Detroit is surrounded by lakes and waterways so it already feels like an island, and when those waters would freeze over I'd feel walled in. When the sun dropped at 5 p.m. each day, I'd begin to long for things that feel unnatural and unattainable, like racing through the Sonoran Desert on horseback or appreciating in person the intricate beauty of the Mexican Elstreak butterfly or staying stoned for long days on a warm beach down in Mozambique, even though I was never a stoner or a butterfly enthusiast or a fan of riding around on horses.

Those unattainable longings drove me to drink more, and earlier in the day too, and became my normal. Move to Detroit when you're already in the dumps and the outcome is a foregone conclusion. I was drawn to this city. I moved here from Phoenix for a journalism gig at the *Detroit Weekly*. But I also moved here because the city to me is absolutely, breathtakingly beautiful. It's a city so bent on demonstrating to anyone who'll notice that no matter how great something is all that is created within it will crumble and die. It's absolutely godless.

It didn't take long for entropy and loneliness of the city to creep in, and when it did it ping-ponged inside my skull like the yap of a freezing bulldog in an abandoned factory.

When I came to, the apartment was freezing. I could see my breath. Jenna was snoring quietly beside me and I could see her breath too. The last night's sleet had turned to snow, which was casting in drifts on the streets below. A horrible storm with gale-force winds had obviously blown through. It didn't help that one window was busted out, and the cardboard that we had duct-taped over the broken part got blown out in the storm, which let in the freezing wind and snow and sleet. You could see frost on the insides of the windows now, and on the red brick walls near those windows. There was snow on the floor beneath that busted window, which we broke out one night when we were drunk and fighting. Well it was Jenna who actually broke it. She threw a metal folding chair at me and I got out of the way and it smashed through the window and went down five stories with all the glass to the sidewalk below and blew apart into a half-dozen pieces. Anyone walking the sidewalk could've really been injured.

The heat must've gone out in the apartment because it was too cold in there for just the busted-out window. That cold air seeped into my bones and I was shivering and my teeth chattered. My fever was through the roof. I tried to separate myself from my head, my brain, which was now beginning to boil over with startling scenes involving decapitated people and run-over animals. I puked over the side of the bed and blacked out.

Jenna's screaming jerked me awake.

"Julian Grayling! Oh, my God. We need to get you to the hospital. *Now!*"

"What …"

There was blood all over the bed. I moved to sit up and my head felt like it'd been split with an axe. My reflection in the window opposite the bed, against the ghostly half-abandoned gray skyline of downtown Detroit, showed a face covered in blood. It came from my nose and mouth. I could understand why Jenna was horrified.

It's never a good sign when drinking causes you to throw up blood, but since I'd done it before I didn't panic so much this time. Really, it just felt like an alcoholic's rite of passage or something. My drunken friends in Los Angeles know all about this kind of thing. Know all about the yellow skin, the weaknesses, the shakes, the ungodly fears.

I'd known for months that my liver had surrendered. I didn't want to believe it. I didn't want to stop drinking either, nor could I. Drinking was necessity. It was no longer fun when I realized I was a drunk who'd get the DTs if I'd go too many hours without booze. I can sort of remember when it hit me that my alcoholism had progressed to the point that I'd get those nervous shakes, the churning in my gut. I'd been drunk everyday of my life for years, only skipping a day or two because I was too sick (from drinking), and even then I'd still manage to get some beer down. But the real scary heebie-jeebies didn't kick in until much later in my drinking life, probably in my 15th year.

Drinking was fun again when I met Jenna. But once I removed the addictive intoxication of the adrenaline that comes with new love, there's nothing left for the alcohol to do. I mean, I needed the booze to be brave with the woman, and then to heighten all the love and lust sensations and everything that goes with that. Once those new-love intoxicants sort of flatline, I was left with the disgusting pallor and jaundice of drink and the havoc that it'd wreaked on my system in the years leading up to that moment. But for a few months I was allowed to forget all about that because I was flower-eyed in love—a feeling no one ever thinks will sour. Booze euphoria is exactly what finding a soulmate feels like. Love and booze always felt the same, at first.

My liver felt heavy in my gut, like somebody had surgically inserted a rubber hot-water balloon just above my stomach. I could feel my liver constantly pushing my stomach down, making it smaller. And it was really tender. It hurt to touch the skin area around where my liver was located. My pallor had gone yellow, or greenish-yellow, depending on the light. I had a low-level fever that never went away. At 35 years old I was calling myself Old Yeller whenever I'd look into a mirror.

I had to stop drinking. It was stop or die. And right there on the bed I made a pact with myself. I said three words to myself: *Today is the day when I finally quit drinking.* Well that's more than three words, but I could barely count. It felt like three words, anyway. It was a promise, which usually meant it was a lie. *But not this time, goddammit.*

———

Jenna was pacing the apartment. She was pretty hungover but she had already managed to get up and out of the bed and make coffee. She dressed up warmly, looked like some kind of Eskimo moving around the loft, big coat, scarf, gloves, bomber hat. She duct-taped the piece of cardboard back over the broken window and she called the landlord about the heat. It was an old steam-heated building so when it went out everyone in the building froze. The landlord promised we'd be warm again by 6 p.m. Outside it was gray and cold, but the snowing had stopped. The wind howled.

Jenna had also changed the sheets around me, and used a warm washcloth to wipe the blood from my face, neck and hair. She used the washcloth on my chest, in long slow caresses from my belly button top to my Adam's apple, and for a minute I thought of her as my mother. I could barely move. Then Jenna slipped me into sweatpants and a long-sleeved shirt and a sweater. She covered me back up in blankets. She mopped the blood and vomit up off the floor. She fed me toast, some of which I even managed to get down. She tried coffee but there was no way I could swallow it. I told her that I was going to be all right, and that she needn't worry.

She paced some more. And then she turned on the TV and crawled under the blankets and wrapped her body around mine. My skin stung to the touch like it was sunburned. It was dark out when the heat came back on in the apartment, and I drifted off.

Jenna could drink but she wasn't a drunk like me. I was seven years older and had been drinking nonstop since I was 17, since I quit bicycle racing to front a punk band. I replaced the high of endorphins of a grueling sport with the easy simplicity of alcohol. I knew I'd found my medicine with that very first bottle of Bud.

It got to the point where each day in the early afternoon my nervous system would light up. My blood pressure would rise and I'd get really scared and anxious if lots of alcohol wasn't handy, so I learned to always keep beer around. On some days that'd be tricky because I'd be counting coins to pay for it.

That's when I developed a taste for malt liquor. I'd freak out if I even thought I wouldn't have enough to get me through the night. I always managed to get it — of course I did — even when I was sleeping on a friend's couch and had nowhere else to go. I was a cliché.

And beyond how beat up I'd feel physically, the guilt and shame bummed me out. No one plans on the career of sinking alcoholic.

I opened my eyes to a world of rising panic. I had the shakes and hissing in the ears. Any doctor or old-timer alchy will say a white-knuckle detox is never a smart idea. You can die that way. By 9 p.m. I was pretty twitchy, scared, sick and hallucinating. Jenna was watching *The Simpsons*. I tried my best to focus on that. It was the episode where Dr. Hibbert runs over Snowball II, the family cat, killing it. Later, Homer tries to win Bart's love by building a robot to fight other machines in a contest. But he stumbles on the construction of it so he puts himself inside the robot and makes it to the final round in the tournament. He gets hurt, loses blood, and is sick with a fever. But he wins the contest. It's a bloodletting and Homer is rewarded with Bart's affection, and he finds real satisfaction.

I kept seeing my mother as Homer's robot. At one point the robot turned to me and I saw myself moving in and out of the television. I was in a Catholic church, a cassock-robed altar boy assisting Father O'Leary, the priest at St. Francis de Sales in Tucson, Arizona, where I really was once an altar boy. We were standing in front of the congregation. My mother, dressed as the robot, stepped out of the TV and cut in front of the line waiting for the rite of Communion. She removed the robot head and I saw myself holding the gilded bread plate under her chin.

The ruddy-faced O'Leary pulled a Eucharist wafer off his paten, offered it up with his right hand and said, "The body of Christ." My mother opened her mouth and took the wafer on her tongue, swallowed it and said, "Amen." She then turned to me. Her eyes narrowed into points and her face suddenly shifted into a horned demonic creature and she scowled with stinking hot breath, "What in the hell are you doing *here*? You don't belong here." Suddenly the TV sucked in the whole horrifying scene and I was standing beside Homer who was drinking a martini and crooning a Bobby Goldsboro tune. My alcohol joneses kicked into higher gear and my entire body shivered and I was jackknifing blankets off of my legs, off of the bed. It felt like car-battery jumper cables were clamped to my calf muscles. I remember hoping I'd hit my head and knock myself unconscious.

This was the worst trauma I'd ever experienced. "This is so fucked up! You need to get to a fucking hospital, you asshole. Let me call an ambulance. …"

Jenna was right. I should've gone to a hospital. I managed to explain to her that I'd detoxed before and that this will only last "a short time." In my delirium I was still trying to minimize my alcoholism. I was embarrassed. Only sick people go to hospitals.

I'd been able to hide the shakes from Jenna. I never wanted her to know. I wanted her so bad. She was seeing the real me, and it was coming out blood red.

I wouldn't hide all my drinking from everyone. One reason I got hired at this particular Detroit newspaper was because I drank a lot. They liked that, called me old school.

I'd report to my work, my editors. I'd write the stories. It wasn't easy, man, especially the parts that involved the reporting and the writing, which is basically the whole job. I missed most of the staff meetings because I was either drunk or hungover. I'd drink on the job, if only to quell prickly nerves and hand tremens. A few snorts of whisky from a hidden flask in my shoulder bag would go a long way. I was so cognitively dulled from drinking. Was operating at about 25 percent of my abilities.

It got to the point where I had, give or take, six hours in a day when I'd be relatively okay. I'd show up at work at 11 a.m. and split around five, just as the nerves would fray and the shakes would begin, usually in my pinkies. I balanced my drinking like that for months. But those shakes and that nervousness would sometimes invade earlier in the day, or if I had more than one cup of coffee, and there was never relief, and every drink felt like it was needed like how you need air in your lungs after you've been holding your breath.

Sometimes I'd have to stay in my office all night to finish a 7,000-word feature story. In those instances I'd drink numerous 40-ouncers of King Cobra and Mickey's malt liquor at my desk. The high sugar content in malt liquor provided a bizarre energy that worked for writing stories.

My main editor, James Stott, trusted me though, and I him. He was a churlish guy with a poorly trimmed beard who grew up in the mountains of eastern Ohio.

Stott knew how to separate the corporate side of the *Detroit Weekly*, that is, the advertising side, from its editorial side. He was constantly telling the publisher to fuck off. There was no way he'd allow any advertiser to infect the editorial output. He shielded his writers from anything or anyone that would keep them from reporting and telling the truth. Stott was an ink-stained editor from the old days who came up working at major daily newspapers. I loved him dearly.

When you love and respect someone that much you never want to let them down. But after being on the job for a year it began to feel like my drinking was beginning to let even Stott down. Writing stories while drinking meant that I was drinking on his time, and that made me feel like a liar and a cheat. Sure, we'd go out for drinks and close the bars down — he was, after all, a journalist rooted in tradition — but I'd continue until the sun came up, long after he'd gone home to bed. Stott was the guy who had hired me here, brought me out from Arizona, after I was writing for an alternative weekly there. He knew some about my past in rock 'n' roll and drugs, but just a little of it. I didn't want anybody knowing anything about me; especially the booze and drugs part, my own personal history. He knew that I drank hard, and how I found stories in bars, and I'm pretty sure he hired me based on my abilities as both a writer and a drinker, without knowing just how bad my drinking habits were. It certainly wasn't my résumé that got me hired, because that was shit. I was a drunk and drug addict, and a high-school dropout. Books saved me. Stott gave me a chance. For a guy who rarely doled out compliments, he said that I was a helluva writer. Others did too, I guess. I had that.

But now I had this. By midnight it felt as though I'd been trapped in the precise moment when two cars collide, and the moment repeated over and over. That's the best way to describe it. All skidding tires, screams, shattering glass and burning bodies and it's never going to end. Somehow I understood on a distant intellectual level that I was actually in a bed in Detroit kicking booze, but the terror of that interior loop-of-death was absolutely real. I pissed and shat myself. It took awhile (an hour, an afternoon, a day, two days? — I couldn't tell) to realize that the screaming I was hearing was my own. It felt like the worst dysentery mixed with the cognitive symptoms of a nervous breakdown; my heart pounded, the bed spun and I had to suck hard for air to breathe. It's the kind of panic rooted in a place so dark you couldn't even imagine it existing, within you or without you.

I had no downers, no Valium, no nothin' to ease the joneses and the sickness. I was ill-prepared, like always. That was part of my problem, as Jenna had pointed out on our third night together. I was never thinking ahead, only looking backwards.

I don't know why I just didn't drink right then to fix me. I mean, once you start getting sick it's too easy to get a bottle, which would absolutely obliterate the pain. A life of suffering as an alcoholic is better than the way I felt. I could've called the liquor store around the corner, or the blues club in Greektown, and maybe had someone haul up a case of beer. There was a strip bar on the ground floor of my building. Hell, I could've shouted out the window for a bottle. Someone would've responded for a ten-spot.

I had a view that looked east down Lafayette, past the gaudy neon of the Greektown Casino and the old Saints Peter and Paul Catholic Church, past the lovely Mies van der Rohe-designed townhouses (one of a few buildings left within reasonable distance of historic luxury) to the ruined riverfront of the Detroit River and across to the kempt shoreline of Windsor, Canada. I had another view looking south that showed me downtown. In either direction I could see bars and dead factories. I loved how much of this town was built on blue-collar drinking.

If I made it to the other side I'd have a chance. So I stayed the course and accepted everything that was going on. The blood that came out of my body had really fucked with my head this time.

It took three full days for the bad nightmares and sicknesses to wane. Jenna nursed me the whole way through. I scared her beyond reason and felt horrible about that, on top of how embarrassed I was.

The post-detox after-effects were ugly and pronounced. Fractals twisted all around on the peripheries of my eyesight. It took a few weeks to even begin to feel that line where my skin ended and the world started. The twitches weren't easy to hide when I went back to work on Thursday, five days sober — with a writing assignment due. I'd taken all my sick days, which weren't enough to ride this thing through. I was eating a little though, and feeling a bit better, but I was still a mess of raw nerves and was still imagining things. For instance, I thought someone was trying to deck me. I'd find myself ducking suckerpunches from men who weren't there. Ducking at nothing. When I'd step out of my office, editors and other writers would ask what was up with my sudden bends and twists. I'd say, "Ah, nothing man, just a sharp pain in my side," and shuffle along. It felt like the weight of my own history was manifesting itself into some asshole with mean fists who was then following me around and trying to deck me for attempting to go at life sober. That's how I reasoned it anyway. God I wanted to drink.

I tried to stay out of everyone's eyesight. Thankfully my office was located in the very back of the newsroom, behind giant bookshelves and stacks of old weeklies. I holed up there. I have no idea how I completed the story, one idiot word at a time.

———————————

A couple is doomed if one person sobers up and the other one doesn't. It's easy to become a self-righteous prick when you get sober. But I suppressed the biased judgments of a newly sober asshole as it applied to Jenna or any of my drunken friends. I didn't offer up advice. There was nothing I could say to anyone. To even presume that there was would've made me dishonest. Jenna wasn't ready to stop drinking when I was. That's it.

The insides of gutted bars and cynical barstool banter with like-minded drunks and rock and rollers were suddenly replaced by A.A. meetings in moldy, fluorescent-lighted basements of old Detroit churches and soothing conversations on folding chairs with the old black ladies in church hats. I listened to those ladies. I learned from them. It was confusing and challenging and nothing ever felt at home like how a barstool feels at home.

Jenna wasn't exactly in sympathy with my sobriety. She was throwing a drunken party to herself nightly, and it was the same party she was throwing to herself when we met, only I was no longer invited. It ain't easy to sit and watch a party to which you're not invited, one thrown by the beautiful woman you'd fallen in love with.

"You're just a fucking student of some stupid tragic destiny," Jenna said one night when she was hammered and I wasn't. "That's all you are."

I was trying my best in my mind to invent a future and not allow my history to intrude and dominate. And I knew deep down that if I stuck it out with Jenna I would certainly start drinking again and likely die. I also knew I didn't have the strength to leave her. That would be like jumping off the mighty Ambassador Bridge into the frigid, dark Detroit River.

After I detoxed, Jenna stayed sober for two weeks, bless her heart. I guess she figured that I'd begin drinking again soon. I figured I would too. But I didn't, one day without booze begat another. The detox itself was so frightening it actually helped me stay straight.

But I'll give Jenna credit: instead of sneaking drinks, she'd ask if it was okay to get some wine for herself. I loved her so of course I said it was fine. My fair-mindedness surprised me, because I was hardly that way drunk. Now I was passive and indecisive. But for her, one bottle meant three. Soon she was sloshed by 9 p.m., nightly. It worked out okay, at first.

I spent most of those early sober weeks and months watching movies every night until I was bug-eyed. Movies were quick and easy diversions from drinking, and they're highly addictive when you're not feeling much and you don't want to feel much. But I would get a panic in my gut if the pickings were slim and we couldn't find anything to watch. In such desperate moments I'd settle for Steven Seagal because even *Under Siege* had Tommy Lee Jones and Gary Busey and was still better than the fear that fuels the desire to get hammered.

At home we watched pretty much every foreign movie, every indie flick, every vintage film that Detroit's only Blockbuster Video had available.

Some nights we'd triple up. Once we watched Roman Polanski's *Repulsion*, Disney's *The Parent Trap* with Hailey Mills, and *Dirty Mary Crazy* Larry starring the awesome Vic Morrow, Peter Fonda and the sexy-dirty Susan George. My stomach swirled when George appeared on the screen, just as it did when I was nine years old, the first time I saw the movie.

I felt the same heady little crush that I had on her then. She must've represented longing for something from my childhood, some kind of innocence that needed to be tarnished.

Luckily we watched *The Parent Trap* last. Hailey Mills was great because her doe-eyed performance fully squashed the unexpected mind-fuck of *Repulsion*. With its horrific walls-come-alive hallucinations and Catherine Deneuve's descents into madness, *Repulsion* hit me as a perfect allegory of alcoholism — that slow fall and how it captured visually what detoxing from booze can be like.

Jenna and I would go out to movies sometimes but that was difficult because, aside from the theater inside the Detroit Institute of the Arts, there are no movie theaters within Detroit. We had to drive miles to a multiplex in the suburbs, which was a drag because the old Ford Escort was a bummer in winter, sober driver or no.

I stayed out of the bars, which made it difficult to actually work because it was inside of those bars where I'd find stories for the newspaper. I didn't know how to work without the bars, without the people I'd meet there and stories I'd hear while drinking. My editor Stott noticed that too. He called me into his office one day to talk of the fact I'd quit drinking. He said getting sober was a "really a good thing, something that would encourage any other journalist to step up their game."

I inhaled and told Stott that I saw myself as clichéd part of a strain of drunken journalists whose sole professional survival depended on the old working-class bars of the world, like those found on nearly every street corner in Detroit.

"I agree," he said.

"But those very bars have gotten the best of me."

He nodded. But it was a slow, observational nod, which made

me nervous. It told me that maybe his empathy only extended so far.

"Look," he said, "I can drink and I can get my work done. If you can't, and if this involves extenuating circumstances, then ... " he paused and shook his head. He added, "I think it's great that you're off the bottle, but don't let that actually hinder your abilities as a journalist. In some ways I guess you're even more of a journalist than I thought."

"Um, what do you mean?"

"I mean that piece that you did on the traffickers turning out the Ukrainian prostitutes is going to win every journalism award there is. What I'm trying to say is do you think you would've been able to find or do that story while sober?"

Good question, I thought. That story was tough to do. It involved getting an address and trailing a handful of Ukrainian mooks from Detroit to New Jersey and back in the dead of winter. I wrote how they drove out to Newark to pick up a bunch of young women and brought them back to Detroit. They put them up in a gated house in Huntington Woods outside of the city and prostituted them out. A few of the girls even wound up working Michigan Avenue near Dearborn among the strip bars. I got a couple of them talking, and told their stories.

The piece sparked a federal investigation and the whole prostitution ring got popped. But I was terrified. I thought the Ukrainians were going to kill me. One day I found a bullet in a package with no return address sent to me at work, and someone used baseball bats to beat the shit out of my Ford Escort (but it still ran OK). The paper put me on ice in a hotel for two weeks "for my own safety. Until the cops can sort this thing out."

Now that I was off the booze, it's telling to remember that I was completely drunk the whole time I did that story. I was even drinking on the drive to and from New Jersey. I had a freelance photographer with me, a straight guy everyone called "Sweet Cheeks," who did most of the driving. He wouldn't shut up about how much alcohol I consumed. He finally shut up on the return trip, somewhere in Pennsylvania, but not before telling me that he couldn't wait to get away from me, and that I was "the most unprofessional motherfucker" that he'd ever worked with. There was no arguing with that assessment. I felt terrible about being such a sloshy downer.

But later, after Sweet Cheeks had read my story, he called to tell me that never in his life did he even imagine that a drunk could write so well, and he called me a real motherfucker. I loved that he said that. He swore he wouldn't tell my editors about my drinking. I reminded him that I was indeed a pro, "a pro drinker, that is."

And I got hip to that hooker story at the Detroiter, a downtown tavern. I was manning a barstool and eavesdropping on a lame conversation between two middle-aged white guys with Fantastic Sams hair and beer guts who just got out of a Red Wings hockey game. They talked drunkenly about shooting phone porn with Ukrainian hookers in Southfield. It sounded so obvious and banal at first. But then I befriended them, and we drank beers and wound up talking about the porn. I got a phone number or two and things began to play out from there. That's an example of how stories evolve from drunken conversations on barstools.

"I guess what I'm saying is that whatever makes you good in the game is the very thing that kills you in the everyday," Stott said.

"The bottle does hit back," I said.

"Well, I will say that in my experience, only the best journalists ever reach that point."

"Uh, thanks," I said.

His comment had me feeling depressed about not drinking. And so it felt like my days at the paper were numbered, which made me panic. Journalism was now my life. I began to realize that I was hired on at the *Detroit Weekly* as the token barfly to track down stories that are nearly impossible to find anywhere but in a bar. They cut me slack because of it. No other reporter or writer was allowed to show up for work at 1 p.m.

Every soul on a barstool has a story that they'll share when they're oiled up, bullshit booze-speak or not. But you need to be drinking with them to get the stories otherwise you'll never establish trust with that person. I'm talking about the hard-luck yarns that make feature-length stories interesting. And that's what I did; I told magazine-length stories featuring people on the fringes. I felt more at home with those folks than anyone else. I once told a love story between a one-armed prostitute and a decorated alcoholic war vet who were on their last skids. I traveled with a couple of gambling-addicted repo men, from all-night repossessions to the sunrise casinos. I had a mid-level crack dealer take me to all his stops in the city, in the back of a cab, only to have him pull a gun on me when I took his picture. I told that one in first person and it made a great story and got a huge following. I left all the drinking stuff in but changed the name of the dealer. I did lots of these kinds of stories.

But no more. Not sober. If I was hearing my editor correctly, I needed to drink to keep my job.

The A.A. meetings were warm and comforting once I got

past the judgmental doctrine of the 12 steps. To me, the entire program is based on cult-speak, fear motivation and conformity. The 12 Steps is about admitting that you're completely out of your mind, and that you are basically powerless to do anything about it. Therefore you're not responsible for yourself. It's about surrendering to some god. It's a stale and dated technology that overloads leverages on your worst insecurities about being a loser and then it hooks you on the belief that some made up spirit will fix your head and restore your sanity. A.A.'s founder, incidentally, used A.A. to pick up chicks and lie and cheat on his wife. There's your spiritual guru.

But the meetings helped me stay sober and they reinforced other ideas involving the greater good, such as simple compassion toward others. For me they were all about the old ladies in the church hats. I found a meeting in the basement of an old church off Livernois near Davison that saw a number of these elderly women, these Southern-born octogenarian matriarchs who offered me shoot-straight wisdom. They became my personal gods. The meeting itself became my home group and it had 20 to 30 regulars each week, mostly old-timers — a mix of retired auto-factory rats and educators and ex-street urchins. As far as I could tell, I was the only white person who ever attended.

One woman of 80, Gurvene, told stories of segregation and years of living in poverty. She had a husband and son when the 1967 Detroit riots broke out. They lived just off Clairmont near ground zero. Her husband was killed during those riots, suffered a skull fracture that was never explained to her.

"The police claimed they looked into it," Gurvene told me once over coffee. "They claimed that. But I will say that you just don't know how long the days can be after something like that happens. You just don't ever know."

She said his body was found in the same spot off West
Grand Boulevard where Paul Williams from the Temptations
had committed suicide six years later. Gurvene told me that
Williams happened to be her first-ever boyfriend. Her husband
was her second. She'd met Williams soon after he'd moved
to Detroit from Alabama, and just before his pre-Temptations
group The Elgins signed to the then-tiny Motown Records.
Williams' suicide was the last straw for Gurvene in that area
of Detroit. After that she moved into a little house on Detroit's
east side to raise her son, but life didn't improve. Crack swept
through their neighborhood.

"Rotted it from the inside out," she said.

Her son was shot in the head in a drug deal gone south. He
was kept alive for a few weeks at St. John's Hospital. That's
when, she said, the whiskey finally got her by the throat.

When I knew Gurvene she was always immaculately turned
out, favoring lavender hats, dark dresses and gloves, which
she removed indoors. My own sobriety felt tiny next to hers;
my suffering felt self-created. Hers was informed by murder,
racism and poverty, things that killed her family and ripped her
city apart. After her son died she lost her house and lived on the
streets for a number of years. Then she found help, got sober,
became a caregiver and now lives alone in a little brick colonial
in a well-kept neighborhood near the University of Detroit
Mercy, just a few blocks from where, she pointed out, Marvin
Gaye and Little Stevie Wonder once lived. She was to me proof
of someone who walked through the hell of living to arrive at a
place where some kind of grace really did exist.

We were drinking coffee around her kitchen table one
afternoon when she zeroed in on me.

"The fear has got you crippled on the inside, son," she said.
I nodded.

"You can't see shit."

I nodded some more.

"You need to retrace those stumbles that led you to my kitchen, young man. There's more to staying off the bottle than grit and endurance, uh-huh."

Then she let out a mischievous cackle and her huge body bounced up and down. It was one of those laughs that could be interpreted in any number of ways. It frightened. Was she laughing with me or *at* me. I never felt so obvious, and white.

She said "blessed" a lot too. It was okay when she said it because it sounded sincere. That word was bandied about daily in Detroit in ways that suggested blind obedience to some authority in the sky. It wasn't offensive, just irritating. A.A. showed me that the attempts to investigate gods or higher powers are valid. But I knew any ways we use to truly understand a god will fail, even if it's only in our hearts. It's what helped me to interpret for my own temporary wellbeing a lot of the pious pabulum found in that program.

Most folks in A.A. found god when they were at their absolute worst and most vulnerable, when they'd nearly wiped themselves out. Once you're shattered and have burned all options, the idea of a savior is mighty appealing, and if you happen to stay sober, then, well, it can't be because of you, now can it?

Booze was supposed to be the reward. You drank because you made it through another worthless day. Soon Jenna was going out for those rewards without me. I'd end up climbing walls, pacing, hurting. Felt cheated on. Panicked. Sometimes she'd step through the door at sunup, disheveled and wasted, having managed to get that Ford Escort home from god knows where. For once it made me angry that Detroit was a city where you could drive around drunk and not get popped. Secretly I'd hoped Jenna would get a DUI. Soon she moved out. The future was black.

But I had Gurvene and other elderly ladies in their Sunday best. Kept them with me as months went by.

One warm evening I took a walk around downtown. It was summertime and the night was wide open and the streets had come alive. It was still light out at 9 p.m. I passed the same bar where Jenna and I had downed hundreds of drinks, where I had found at least a half-dozen feature stories for the paper. Memories resided inside. So I stopped and looked in the window and there she was, sitting all barstool sexy with a straight back, sloshy-happy but with distance in her face. She was the same woman that I'd fallen in love with. I hadn't seen or spoken to her in months. I went inside and she saw me. Her face showed surprise, then anger and resentment. There was no sadness or nostalgia. Knew her well enough to see all that, and it stung. The guy perched beside her glanced at me and got up and moved quickly toward the restrooms. He was big. He must've known who I was. I figured he was just another drunk with a replaceable head.

Jenna looked at me flatly as I approached.

I said, "Is that your new love?"

She nodded slowly, said nothing and pressed her lips together.

I couldn't blame Jenna for shit. It's hard to live, much less embrace, a life seemingly without variation. That's why we bolt from it. I'd been bolting since I was a teenager. Sometimes it's luck to be here at all.

Gurvene reminded me once that it's not about luck. She said luck was nothing more than improved eyesight. The way things exist often depends upon how you read them. For the first time in years I had been moved to tears by a single sunset, one scratched up by power lines and bare-boned trees and tops of derelict Victorians. I saw rewards there, fleeting as they were.

The church hat ladies taught me that nothing really ends; shit just changes. And the changes prepare you for when your heart finally stops beating, at which point you become a pile of compost, stinking and surrounded by flies. The accumulation of a life-long, garbage-in, less garbage-out self study.

I left Jenna there on the stool at the bar. Her new boyfriend was in that bar somewhere but he wasn't revealing himself. I wanted to tell her that I got fired from the *Detroit Weekly*, and that I thought it was pretty funny that I was only as good as my last least-sober story. I really wanted her to know that I loved her and that I was sorry for messing up our plans. Instead I turned and walked out of there sober and disconsolate as my 8th-grade self. On the street outside I saw the blinking lights and walked toward them. They spelled out two, maybe three, words.

Ghosts and Fireflies

Ghosts and Fireflies

Julian dreamed that the summer was over and that he hadn't gone hunting. He'd never hunted before in his life. He hated the idea of hunting and hunters, and he didn't eat meat. But he dreamed of the prey and the shotgun and the open wounds and the death.

He'd dream that he didn't feel anything. Not for Regina or their dog Mott, or for anything at all. Not music or books. It made him feel sick in the dream as though he'd been in prison. Everyday felt like he was in prison with no release date set. He was just there, not doing, not being. He was just there, as if stuck on some cold bunk, staring ahead blankly, consumed by foulness and hardly breathing. And it would only get worse. He knew the feeling itself was hardly a dream.

He returned to the sentences, crossing out those that contained self-pitying bullshit, and then tearing out a whole new sheet from the notebook and starting fresh. When he finished the note he folded it in half and on a blank side wrote "Regina" in larger print. He taped it to the front door of the house. It had instructions to first call 911 and let them deal with it, and to not enter the house because it would be unendurable for her. "Please forgive me, Regina," he wrote.

Then he went and woke up Mott and scooted him off the couch. He put the good boy down in the basement. That was the hardest thing to do. Closing Mott off in the basement. Julian could barely look at him, their border terrier, this giver of undying love and comfort. He closed the basement door on Mott's face and protuberant eyes, which looked up at him with confusion and sadness. Mott must've known, Julian thought, that his owner was fucking shit up, again.

Julian climbed the stairs to their bedroom. He got on his belly and slid under the bed until he found the box way back against the wall. He slid back out pulling the box with him. He went to the bathroom and closed the door. He sat on the cold tiled floor, leaned against the wall opposite the toilet, and carefully pulled the .38 from the box. The gun was heavy and scary and cold in his hands, and without hesitation, as if to deflect second thoughts, he opened his mouth, stuck the gun barrel in and placed his finger on the trigger.

The sky had clouded over on that day and the clouds rolled in over Lake St. Clair. The wind had shifted hard to the north, which put a sting in the air. He could hear the long moans of a foghorn. Earlier in the day he watched two scenery-eating freighters, one a few hundred yards ahead of the other, moving at a snail's pace on the lapping water. The leaves were turning now and the rotted beauty of Detroit, the city that had, in the last few years, abducted his heart, looked alive in so many electric colors. The curve of the shoreline took in the suburbs, and they looked alive too. After a good night's rain the trees, streets and rooftops were stained flame orange and yellow. Everything was slowly receding before him like some half-remembered song, and it was beautiful.

In his mind he watched the graying light darken the trees

behind their house. He saw Regina arrive home in her car after a visit with her sister. She looked happy and he could even smell the cigarettes and wine on her. She moved up the front steps with a kind of mirthful bounce and found the note taped to the front door. She carefully opened the note and read it, and the light drained from her face. She fell against the wall of the house and slid down the side and lay on the concrete porch.

His every muscle contracted and he could no longer move, and it felt like hot water was roiling in his stomach, pumping into his arms and fingers. He thought it odd that his last thoughts before the explosion were not all of Regina, or his siblings, but that of a burly doorman at a horrible Hollywood club where his band had played a miserable show. It was a memory from years ago, and it just floated there in his mind. As Julian eased his finger on the trigger he watched this guy's jowls bounce in a kind of slow motion, saying, "You'll never step into this bar again, asshole."

One night about two years after they'd met, Julian and Regina were driving home after having dinner with her parents. It was Christmastime. They were moving slowly along strings of streetlights, and little else was visible. There was no other traffic out. Giant snowflakes fell from blackness and looped in the headlights.

Julian reached out and cut the volume on the radio and then slid his hand into Regina's. He nodded his head toward the windshield and said, "It's like each streetlight has its own ghost."

Regina smiled faintly and looked out at the streetlights.

"You can see by the halo that hovers above each one," Julian added.

"You're right, Julian," Regina said. "And it is beautiful."

"Those ghosts are from your past," he said. "I see each as a person I knew once, just hovering in the same spot in the freezing cold."

Regina didn't say anything but kept her gaze fixed on the passing lights and the rotating shadows made by the slow cycle of the windshield wipers. They drove along like that for some time. Then Julian said, "Those ghosts call out silently. Sometimes I swear I can hear my dad and my mom."

They came upon a giant blow-up snowman outlined in neon red and green suspended from a tree and Julian pulled their car over to the side of the road.

Regina turned to him. "Why did you stop?"

"Driving through this shit's hard on me," he said, staring up at the snowman and wondering himself why he stopped, and why he chose to stop beneath this snowman, which, in the darkness, appeared to be hanging from a noose.

"What shit is hard?"

"This shit," he said.

"This what?"

"This idea that we all have to be here."

"Be where?"

"Here," he said.

"Here where?"

"Here on this planet."

Regina looked down to her hands folded in her lap. She waited for the apology, which she knew was coming.

"I'm sorry," Julian said a minute later. "That's not what I meant. I didn't mean to sound so sour and self-involve-y."

"It's okay," she said. "I know your shit."

"I know you know."

"You're fictionalizing yourself again," she said.

"Really?

"Yes, Julian. Jesus."

The engine hummed and the windshield wipers went back and forth brushing away the snowfall.

He said, "But my question is how do you negotiate all your fears and all the faces from your history and still have room inside of you to live and participate in the world as it is now? Where do all the ghosts go?"

"What ghosts?"

"All these ghosts," Julian said.

"I'm sorry you see ghosts."

"Do you really think that's what it is?"

Regina leaned over and put her arms around his neck and squeezed. She touched her forehead to his and looked directly into his eyes so that he'd understand her easy-tempered tone when she said, "Why, oh why are you so against yourself all the time?"

"Seriously," Julian said. "I'm sincerely asking, where do you put all the ghosts?"

"The past isn't real," she said. "You can't fix ghosts, they're not here."

"Do you ever think about the miscarriage?"

Regina pulled back upright in her seat, turned to him with a disgusted look and let out a heavy sigh. "No! That was more than a year ago."

"Maybe there's a ghost of a being that in some abstract weird way makes me a father and you a mother?"

"Are you out of your fucking mind, Julian? Stop. Just *stop*."

Julian turned to look at her keeping both hands on the steering wheel. Regina was the first person he'd ever attempted

to establish a life with while not being absolutely shit-faced. She
was his first sober love. And gone with the booze was any sense
of his self-importance; at least that's what he'd hoped. Being
with Regina felt like privilege and that made him nervous,
which made him say stupid things that didn't make much sense.
His foot was often in his mouth.

He wanted to hear her stories. She made him want to say
to her that he was committed. Committed to the challenge of
being responsible, and in the moment, with her. Even when he
was sour, and down. Taking responsibility for his reactions and
committing out loud to being with her, just like how any person
evolved beyond childhood would do.

The sky was big and bright on that day they met. Sailboats
and kites and dogs on leashes, and children with dads getting
their fireworks ready at sunset, waiting for dark on the Fourth
of July, on a ledge overlooking the Little Traverse Bay on
Michigan's Lower Peninsula. It was silly. Regina's sundress
moved with the wind off of the water, and she was actually
licking an ice cream cone when they began talking. And
there was no missing her beauty, all curvy with dark eyes
and perfect skin.

She said her mom was Greek and her dad Irish.

Their first 48 hours together were spent fucking and
listening to Mississippi John Hurt, her favorite. It was so
saccharine-sweet Regina made jokes of Meg Ryan and
diabetic comas.

Julian happened to be there in Harbor Springs, writing a
blowjob piece detailing Michigan vacation spots for a shitty
airline magazine. He needed money, bad. She was there because
some of her art was showing in a local gallery. She hated art
galleries but this showing was an excuse for her to get out of

Detroit for a few days and maybe sell a painting or two.

He'd never met a woman so confident, who somehow moved directly down the center of time and place, where everything lined up and made sense. How'd she do it? That disposition was hard to disrupt. He swore to himself after three days with her that he'd never *ever* disrupt that disposition.

Her parents had taught her about art and culture when she was a girl, had encouraged books and museums. She'd hilariously correct museum docents who'd misstate facts. One time they were at some showing at the Detroit Museum of Art and after much eye-rolling Regina took over some conversation about personal shame that sparked in front of a Max Ernst sculpture. She launched into a sort of tongue-in-cheek scholarly lecture bringing the idea back to guys like Egon Schiele, how you can detect personal and sexual shame in the twists of his nude self-portraits, and she lipstick-traced that up through the 20th century to others, photographer Diane Arbus to Factory girl Holly Woodlawn and porn star Tiffany Minx.

Julian's jaw slacked. How she connected the dots and mocked art academics. She needed to be confident. She earned her living with her art. No trust fund, no rich parents. She was damn good at it, and because of that she was celebrated in certain circles in Detroit, Los Angeles and New York.

Her figurative paintings made people nervous. They had exaggerated gestures and inventive color combinations, with loose-lipped themes and droll eroticized subtexts involving downtrodden women and the queening of men. And they sold. Julian didn't know shit about painting but he recognized deliberate moves to transcend styles and fuck with people's expectations.

Her imagery was both severe and graceful. Sometimes

she shifted gears and tackled weightier themes, pieces that allegorized turmoils forced upon Michigan's Native Americans. In one, soldiers stormed a fright-faced Chippewa family whose legs were crops in the ground. Another saw Native American children sucked into a culture-cleansing existence, floating toward a heaven of dancing whiskey bottles and flat-screen TVs.

Julian returned his gaze to the snow falling on the windshield. He said, "I'm sorry I said that. I hate it when I say stupid shit."

Regina shook her head, smiled slightly, and leaned over and kissed him on the throat. "I'm glad I didn't know you when you were a drunk."

Regina and Julian had been together long enough for her to recognize the exact scent of his depression before it'd lay him out. Even a slight change of light in his eyes would give it away. There was little she could do when that blackness rolled over him but she did her best to inhabit his world, to suffer with him in some humane effort to, maybe, pull him from his depths. She believed in him, and it was selfless.

Julian stepped out of the car bunching his shoulders against the snow and the freezing darkness under that false snowman and walked around to her side of the car. He opened the door and felt the heat from the car's cabin reach his face. She gave him a quizzical look but didn't say anything. He put his hand out and she took it. He pulled her out into the freezing dark and held on to her tight.

His dead dad would return to him daily, in the whistle of freight trains, in the glow of fireflies, in the daily grinds of men he knew who actually worked hard at their jobs because they had mouths to feed. And his wide powerful hands, tall frame and forever five-o'clock shadow. He was a war vet. Even as a kid Julian understood his dad's sense of self-reliance, and he later envied it. And the most striking and obvious thing about his dad was his keen intelligence. He exuded that kind of self-assurance that said he knew the secret to how things work. No question would go unanswered: "Dad, how many days would it take to get to the sun?" "Dad, how do TVs work?" He knew everything.

Julian long ago forgave the childhood beatings. He understood a father saddled with a kind of sensitivity, and a sentimentality, that put him at odds with everyone, from his workplace buds to the men of his generation. Julian's mother didn't much respect what she called Dad's "overly sensitive and passive side" either. She frequently told him as much. That "shortcoming" also guaranteed that people take advantage of him. So Julian's mom betrayed his dad by fucking other men. Those kinds of burdens made easy his dad's drinking and desperate shows of cruelty toward his children. Julian knew his father suffered truckloads of guilt from carrying out such cruelty but it was years before he could begin to unravel with any real insight his dad's emotional roadblocks. And now, remembering the earliest times when things had gone wrong, Julian had undying empathy for his pop. He watched his dad punish himself, outside of the drinking. He'd engage in long hours of obsessive yard work in the hot summer sun. He sweated like a dozen men and his skin burned raw because he'd do the work shirtless, wearing only shorts, and without sunblock. He'd pull weeds from between cacti without protective gloves, attack hedges with dull hand trimmers, and mow the front and back yards using a rusted, antiquated push-mower. He had thick forests of body hair, which was no line of defense against the horrible sun. By evening he'd be lobster red. Sometimes those burns gave up mounds of plasma-oozing blisters on his back and legs, and on the top of his forehead, which, eventually, years later, led to the cancer that killed him. Julian figured it was Dad's way of self-immolation.

When Julian got into his 20s his dad became his favorite person. It took time for the admiration to grow but it hit stride when his dad opened up about "the black dogs of depression," and war wounds and an unfaithful wife who'd been his first love. He talked of things dads didn't talk about. They were difficult conversations too, for both of them. Not a day went by now when Julian didn't wish he could phone up his pop and shoot the shit about writer Edward Abbey or guitarist Charlie Christian or nature conservancy, or his own battles with the bottle, or whatever.

Julian returned to summers, and childhood trips into the pines. The winding roads up to that White Mountain campsite, 10,000 feet above sea level and no one else around. It was always just Dad and the three kids and their little wiener dog Chew with the misaligned teeth and funny underbite. Mom never made those trips.

Monsoon storms would inevitably greet them. Dark clouds moved in above the sandstone slopes of the Mogollon Rim, shooting lightning sideways and thundering their world. Their campsite felt walled in by unmapped landscape, all rising bluffs and thick timber whose lowest branches were still at least 20 feet above their heads. Streaks of light sliced precise angles through the dark shade of deeply fissured ponderosa pines, tall as skyscrapers. Feet crunched on spongy, needled ground. Pinecone brawls between Julian and his big brother Steven left contusions on both of their faces. That portable, army-green stove mixed the smell of burning kerosene with that of the campfire and coffee in bone-freeze mornings. Amongst his bottles of Schlitz, dad placed cans of A&W Root Beer in the cold creek for Julian, Steven and their kid sister Jenn. The stream kept the drinks ice cold.

Julian loved his little hatchet. It fit snuggly in its own holster that he fastened to his belt. He'd wear it with his fake hiking boots and navigate obscure trails through the woods. He'd imagine himself a man, big and physical, a force to be reckoned with, like his pop. He'd take long purposeful steps with a sense of confidence and one hand resting on his hatchet in its holster.

He'd chop up branches found on the forest floor and use them to cook hotdogs and marshmallows in fires built in stone pits. Sometimes a hotdog would fall from the stick into the fire and sizzle and they'd have to dig it from the embers so as not to leave any food that might draw bears to their camp. Chew would get the charred dogs and when he eagerly chomped on them with his deformed little mouth it made everyone laugh and laugh. It was funny every time.

One night they were all asleep inside the tent when a horrific moan shocked them awake. It disorientated and sounded blood thirsty, like anything capable of tearing you to bits. It gripped Julian's stomach and made his body hair stand on end. They listened, terrified, as the ugly thing tore apart the campsite. It was obviously a bear. A hungry bear.

Since the first night of that trip, Julian had snuck his holstered hatchet into his sleeping bag when he crawled in for the night. He had to sneak it in there because Dad wouldn't have approved of a hatchet in a sleeping bag. Tonight he slid the hatchet from its holster and lifted it close to his chest and pounding heart. To Julian, and his brother and sister, the bear meant impending death.

They lay stiff in their sleeping bags. Stiff until words from Dad soothed. He said, "You kids need to be a little quiet because we don't want that cow tipping over the trash and charging in here to find out who was doing all that talking!"

His tone was hushed. Julian had never heard it like that before. It had warmth, offered protection. Julian wasn't scared anymore.

"It doesn't sound like a cow, dad!" Jenn whispered through her missing front teeth.

"It's only a cow," Dad said.

"Where's Chew?" Steven whispered.

"He's here with me," Dad said. "Now hush!" Chew didn't so much as growl, which was odd. Chew would bark at farts and clouds. Dad was keeping him quiet somehow.

Julian closed his eyes clutching the hatchet to his chest, listening to Dad repeat, "It's only a cow." He concentrated on the silence in the dark beyond the noises inside their campsite until the entire world itself was silent. Julian couldn't tell if that silence was real or imagined. His grip on the hatchet loosened, his trembling waned. He finally drifted to sleep. When he opened his eyes again sunlight filled the tent and everyone was still in their sleeping bags. Dad was snoring. Julian could hear the scurrying feet of little unseen animals outside their tent going through the mess that was made of their camp during the night. He was overjoyed to discover that he wasn't torn to shreds by a bear, that no one was torn to shreds by a bear.

Julian found himself lately thinking about that episode, and each time he'd cry. It wasn't the nostalgia that got him, it was the realization of his father's intent — his dad was showing him to live outside of his fear.

In his mind he watched Regina steady her breathing and step through the front door of their house. Hand over her mouth and crying. She moved through the front room and stopped, pulled her phone from the rear pocket of her jeans and hit his number. She followed the ringing up the stairs to their bedroom.

She first noticed his shoes and then his jeans, and she could tell that his phone was ringing in his front pocket. He was wearing the cowboy shirt with the turquoise snaps. Her first thought was that he'd started drinking again, and this whole thing was a sick joke, and he'd missed the bed when he passed out, and the fucking bastard was pretending not to hear that she was calling him. Then she saw the blood. It splayed up the wall and ceiling like a horrible shadow. Her phone skidded across the hardwood floor toward him as she fell to her knees. Then she collapsed.

God he didn't want to hurt her. He also didn't want to hurt her anymore. He had reasoned in his head that she'd be better off in the long run with him out of the picture. He told himself again and again that his death would add specific depth and wisdom to her life experience. He was convinced she'd be better off. He reasoned on that very idea for days, until there was no believing otherwise.

He'd written in the note that he couldn't drag her down any longer and that she could now go on with her life unencumbered by his "wayward mental dawdles and drawn-out periods of selfish depression and suicidal aspirations." And that he was "absolutely bankrupt of intellectual activity and creativity," things that he never cared to admit out loud. The idea that he was an actual inspiration in this woman's existence was to him a tragedy of epic proportion.

There was a point beyond which things only got worse for Julian. Regina thought hard about what that exact point was. Julian believed that he didn't deserve her. Sometimes his guilt about being so transparently wounded would eat at him until he'd stumble on his words in conversations with her and feel like a dipshit. He'd dismiss his depression as nothing more than personal theater crammed with goosed-up melodrama, and leave it at that. When he'd really attempt to define out loud his own troubled world his voice sounded small, like a little kid. It was a fight for him to be anything but a downer. He'd partake in that internal battle when he was alone with her, or on rare occasions when he was with groups of friends. It took incredible effort and force of will to even be present with groups of people, much less alone with Regina, or do things like go for walks, things he'd previously done instinctively. He was consumed by thoughts of suicide, but pulled back by thoughts of her.

He talked of the torture of his future, where he saw himself solely supported by the same tiny freelance writing gigs that were now barely keeping him afloat — that little feature here, that little album review there — and the self-promoting hustle needed to even get those things published. He hated to exist in a culture created and ruled by self-promoters. Lately he only looked forward to certain things, such as twilight, the sundown, because then the treachery of the day would be on its way out. "Night means a potential for regeneration," he'd tell her. Before getting sober he'd celebrate that regeneration with drinking and songs. Now he took an even more insular road and developed habits that included watching old cop-procedurals and reading novels about irredeemable fuckups.

She never could count on him for much. It seemed like an insurmountable task for him to take their car in for an oil change. She was appalled to learn that he hadn't been to a dentist since he was a teenager. Getting him to go was a whole other nightmare. He just couldn't go to the grocery store and get dog food, even after he'd promise that he would.

Though he'd try. Once he got in the car headed to Kroger's for Mott's food, but returned an hour later empty-handed, and the dog was hungry. All Julian could say was that he made it to the grocery store parking lot and sat there, at first stunned by an old song that came on the radio, and then he said he couldn't face the people, the store, the products. He just sat there, frozen. And then he came home. Regina was dumbfounded.

She grew flustered (if not fascinated) by the bleak contrast between his affections for the beauty of the world around him, the very things he talked about, and sometimes wrote about, and the total lack of affection for himself. He was so acutely aware of his own tiny place in the world. It was the realization that he'd experience very little of it. She was amazed how one person could embody all of that. But she never considered that maybe his seemingly relentless pursuit of unhappiness didn't have any sort of meaning. And she never took it personally.

Anti-depressants worked until they wouldn't. Each time he'd try out a new one the consequences would be the same. He'd start a new prescription and after weeks of horrible, anxiety-ridden side-effects there'd be some relief. He knew the drugs were working full-steam when it'd be hard as shit to achieve, much less sustain, a hard-on. And all of his sensations flat-lined and he'd begin to ignore life's small wonders — all those ghosts and fireflies.

The happy pills provided a bent sense of security. Made it okay to tolerate, or maybe even slightly enjoy, the life of some dude who didn't do much but go to a job, come home and be contented with unchallenging, unchanging things, a little house with a tired garden, a failing marriage and weak sobriety and an unhealthy TV habit. There was no creating of anything. No music. No writing. Yet the happy pills ensured a warm and safe shelter from the exterior world, and if you're a suicide case trying to stay sober, that's pretty much right where you want to be.

He also knew the drugs were working when discovering what was broken about himself became less and less a question until it didn't matter. Then he'd be dead inside and sluggish in the head. He'd begin that slow, deadened slog back onto that cold bunk. Then he'd be forced to restart the cycle of switching meds all over again. He couldn't stand to be himself when he lived like that. The idea of suicide would begin to gnaw inside of him. Suicide became a purposeful, silent ambition. Sometimes suicide was a goal.

Because he had no health insurance, switching meds was a pain, the last thing you wanted to do when you were broke and bummed out. It involved dealing with a Canadian pharmacy for prescriptions. Prescription drugs across the border cost a fraction of those in the states. Julian loved that the Canucks can't find one good reason to overcharge their sick and dying. He'd have to mail or fax his script in and wait for the drugs to arrive via the U.S. Postal Service. In the meantime, he'd hear back from the pharmacy with a request to speak to his doctor. Julian would have to get his shrink (who continued to treat him for free long after his insurance had run out) to phone up the

Canadian pharmacy to guarantee that Mr. Julian Grayling was indeed his patient and that the pharmacy did indeed have a legitimate script with his personal signature on it. It was never easy getting his shrink on the phone, and it was even more of a chore for Julian to ask a favor from someone who was already treating him for free. It was so much easier, and cheaper to just buy beer, or crystal meth, or coke.

One day he decided to wean himself off a cocktail of the max dosage of Cymbalta (120 mg a day) and the max dosage of Bupropion (450 mg a day). His doctor agreed that Julian should combat his demons without the happy pills. He said that kind of warfare builds self-esteem. The doc told Regina that he was happy with Julian's progress. Coming off happy pills produced horrible dreams not unlike mild booze withdrawals.

When off the meds his mind would slowly begin to buzz of loss. Everything would feel like loss. The buzz was a consistent whirr beneath his every thought and action, so all of his memories, both the good and the horrible, were tinted in the same sort of grim hue. *Back to normal,* he'd say to himself. No way to rise from the torture of the present, the torture of the day-to-day.

Once, when Julian was three years old, he attempted to define that very sensation to his mother. It's his earliest memory. They were in the kitchen of their little brick house in Tucson, Arizona. He was holding his hand up to her and crying. He remembered a sinking feeling. One likely brought on by the pitiless afternoon sunlight that slanted in through the kitchen window. The light made everything sharp and ugly, the pale lime-green walls and fading daisy-print wallpaper and fake wood grain. At that age he couldn't begin to articulate, much less comprehend, such hopelessness.

He saw himself dead for two months. Saw Regina at her sister's house up in Rochester, sifting carefully through a small box of his things that her sister had collected from his desk. Regina was hungover, two or three bottles of cheap cabernet and a pack of smokes — Marlboro Reds — from the night before. That was her nightly diet, pretty much since his suicide.

Regina hadn't been back to their house yet, and she never would. It was too painful to even drive anywhere near their old neighborhood. But the landlord had been making noises about reclaiming the property, even though he'd given her a free month's rent and said that, in "light of the tragic circumstances," it was "quite alright" if she broke the lease, adding, "of course there would be no penalty."

She'd figured that once she moved out (or once her friends and sister had moved her things out), the landlord would give the little two-bedroom place with a guest house — which she had converted into her painting studio — a fresh coat of paint and then stick out the For Rent sign. The same For Rent sign that Julian and Regina spotted while driving down that tree-lined street more than two years ago. They'd fallen in love with the little two-story brick house with the real plaster walls and hardwood floors, and the rent was affordable, and they wanted out of Detroit City.

Now there'd be no horror story attached to the house. The house would go on. Life would begin anew for some other young couple or struggling single mom, and there'd never be mention of the previous lives that existed between those walls, the hurts and monotonies, as well as all the love. That place on Arcadia Street in St. Clair Shores was still just another house with a half-finished basement and a front and backyard filled with green things that grew no matter what, all within walking distance of an ugly brick church, an elementary school and a lake whose view showed a distant shoreline of a foreign country.

The box contained his laptop, a couple of half-defaced novels that he took everywhere with him, some pencil doodles on notebook paper, a horseshoe from Greece and a little Mexican statue of St. Monica, and weird little keepsakes that he'd collected on their trips up to northern Michigan. He loved northern Michigan. She picked up the smooth, nature-polished Petoskey stone. Its honeycomb pattern suggested anything was possible, he told her, because it reminded him of how bees are givers of life. She saw the joy on his face when he'd discovered that stone. It was on that second weekend they'd spent up north, three weeks after they'd met.

She laughed about how he never really understood the Great Lakes. How he said the lakes were so large and they never did anything but "they did everything." Odd wonders awed him, like the abandoned factories and paper mills in haunted seaside towns such as Ontonagon and Muskegon. The giant maple leaves and a green countryside that bended and shifted against itself with the seasons. And fishing. He never understood fishing either, and he never fished in his life. He never even ate fish. But he loved fishermen and their stories and the act of fishing. He once spent an afternoon grilling one old fisherman on some antiquated pier on Tawas Bay on the delicacies of musky baits and how to target walleye and steelheads. When he climbed back into the car that day, he announced that he was going to become a fisherman, and would she still love him if he became a professional fisherman? He was dead serious.

Regina placed the stone back into the box. She examined a

weirdly curved, sharp-edged pinecone that he'd kept because he liked how it looked "like a distressed bear's dick," and that creepy fist-sized snowman with a tiny fedora and an evil grin that someone fashioned from wood and metal decades ago. Julian found the snowman one summer half buried in the brush near a Lake Michigan beach. His theory, he told her, was that a kid passenger on a ship that had gone down ages ago in Lake Michigan had lost the snowman when he drowned. He had clung on to it until the bitter end. Julian said it was the last gasp of a heart filled with hope.

She dug in the box and found a handwritten gratitude list. Julian would do them a few times a week. He read the notes to himself each morning, quietly, in the bathroom mirror. It embarrassed him and he tried to keep the notes a secret. But she snuck a listen sometimes.

The note:

1. Grateful I'm sober still.

2. Grateful for Regina. She teaches me to recognize oddities of depressed moments. And how those moments rob the joys and beauties that allow hearts to beat … as corny as it sounds.

3. Grateful for any moment of inner peace.

4. Grateful that technology hasn't yet fully yanked me from reality. Like the trees and the weird wonders on lakeside walks; those tiny sounds and furies, and rhythms, inside nature's little hum, and life in present tense.

5. Can't think of fifth one today! Fuck me!

She pulled Mott close, recalling how in the days leading up to his suicide an unknown energy had illuminated Julian's limbs, inserted bounce into his step, and he'd actually said funny things again. And that made-up little dance he'd do, in the bedroom, bare-ass naked, a bizarre kind of Appalachian jig or something, where he'd bounce in place, tossing his limbs about, no music playing. He'd look like an apoplectic stick figure. She'd laugh until her stomach hurt. When Julian gave of himself, when it was obvious he was expending mental and emotional energy in her direction, there was nowhere on earth she'd rather be than with him.

She knew she should absolutely hate Julian right now. She thought of this busted man-boy who wasn't from Michigan, but from that desert town near Mexico. But he had managed to restore himself, away from the self-medication. That's what made her love him unconditionally. He'd been sober for six years. Even his friends were shocked, took to calling him "fortress" for staying sober.

She felt the warmth of his fingertips brushing hair from her forehead.

———

Sometimes Regina would go drinking with friends and stay out late. He couldn't understand why he'd grow frantic, as if she'd never return. He'd struggle to hold panic at bay so it wouldn't mutate into that unlivable terror that was so long ago informed by ugly incidents involving drug and sex addicts and his own addictions. But that's all history and ghosts. Regina was no alcoholic, and just because he couldn't go to bars without feeling the desire to drink didn't mean she should have to avoid them with her friends.

Theirs wasn't a loveless connection. It was the opposite. He knew that much. She would have ditched him long ago otherwise. At the very least that was enough. There was a part of him that knew that maybe she was right about him all along, and that the faulty wiring inside his head insured that his beliefs were at best distortions of fact, and that maybe he chose unhappiness over happiness simply because it offered much heavier doses of pure sensation. Once an addict, always an addict, right?

Motherfucker!

Julian pulled the .38 from his mouth and placed it back inside the box. He put the lid on the box, carried it to the bedroom and slid it back under the bed, where it would remain, like an unhappy song. Then he remembered Mott locked down in the basement. He jumped up and stepped quickly down the stairs to let him out. Mott wagged and yelped and hopped in little circles around Julian's legs. He could barely contain his enthusiasm.

Julian went to the door and retrieved the note that he'd taped there and tore it up into tiny pieces and stuck the pieces into an empty Diet Coke can and flattened the can with his foot and buried it in the trash. Then he made a pot of coffee and sat and drank a cup at the kitchen table. He wished he could phone up his dad, explain things, and let the sound of his voice and words soothe. He'd let his father do all the talking. Julian would listen hard. Regina would be home soon.

Sirens

Sirens

Mad songs of fire and disfigurement drown out the rattle of the evaporative cooler. Any closer and they'd shake the chain-link out front. But they're a few blocks away, looping in the hot June air, assigning a tingly unease to the late morning. Then they stop. The sirens always stop close by.

Cassidy hears them too and looks up from the mess she has created of Tiffany's head. Her little sister sits patiently on the dinette chair placed in the shade, just outside their front door. Her feet swing back and forth, dirty-bottoms almost touching the gravel driveway of mostly engine-drip stains and yellow-flower weeds. She ignores the sirens, and her big sister's brush and scissor work, and concentrates on her lap, finger-tracing the flower prints on her dress. She's a fine customer in this salon.

The girls live in the low cinderblock apartment across the driveway. Cassidy is 11, and she's pretty, with a sharp, short nose, big forehead and that kind of sun-browned desert-rat skin that looks dirty when it's clean. Her hair's nearly the same color, only lighter, and it flows past her shoulders, but today it's pulled back carefully at the sides and held in place by two bobby pins decorated with flowery clusters of fake pink pearls. Her blue eyes highlighted by dark circles underneath. There's a kid's lightness in her step — with a hint of middle-school hipsway creeping in. She's dressed in short cutoffs and a purple t-shirt with a sunflower print.

Tiffany's five years younger and is, I imagine, Cassidy at that age. She's learning to be Cassidy who's learning to be her mom. She sees a world filled with icky insects and funny-looking neighbors, who blare classic-rock radio, stay up late and pitch freshly drained Old Milwaukee cans onto weedy rectangles of dead Bermuda grass from their tiny two-chair porches. Mom and Dad scream at each other almost every night and their faces get stretched out and ugly. She curls herself up in the dirt between the front bushes and the wall, in the dark with all those icky insects.

Some days I read to the girls in my front yard, out in the sun. I select stuff my dad gave me, like Twain or Salinger.

"What does 'enrapture' mean?" Cassidy asks one afternoon, sitting close enough so that she can rest her chin on my forearm.

"It means to fill you up with delight."

"Oh."

"What does 'crisscross' mean?"

"Try pushing your eyes together toward your nose and you'll it."

She tries it. "That's neat," she says.

"What does 'suicide' mean?"

Cassidy turns these little reading sessions into word-question games. She knows she's cute, but she's curious too.

Tiffany stands bright-faced in front of me, legs crossed at her ankles — she rises to just above my head when I sit on the grass — and stares at my eyes, head tilted as she listens.

Yellow-orange Popsicle smear outlines her mouth, and she

never says a word. Like her lips are sealed with sugar.

———————————

Mom adores her daughters. She shows that kind of patience that only comes from love, and the girls make her smile when it looks like she might not ever smile. I've watched them a lot in the two years I've lived here. Some days they'd climb on top of each other and kiss and tell stories on the little brick stoop next to their door. Mom pedaled them on her bike to school and the store. At first Tiffany would ride in the front basket and Cassidy on the child seat over the rear wheel until Cassidy was big enough to wobble alongside on her own little pink bike with handlebar streamers and a flowered banana seat. I'd watch them disappear up the street, all giggles, and Mom pedaling with some difficulty, saddled with so much weight.

Last Halloween Tiffany dressed as a big, fat bee, all yellow and white and black, bouncy antennae. Cassidy was a model, short skirt, skimpy top, smeared makeup. Mom took pictures.

Cassidy already has her guard up, that barrier of detachment that festers when uncommon things happen, self-protection before so many misfires accumulate. Soon she'll discover the differences between her and other girls, and begin to compare exteriors: She'll want to be like them, with pretty new clothes, hairstyles and earrings, streaming music on their phones. She'll want to be desired by boys. She'll want to live in the clean, well-kept suburban neighborhoods, miles from here.

Sometimes I'd talk with Mom. Her name's Serena, and I'd never met anyone with that name. It's a really pretty name, sort of sings when you say it out loud. Thirty-one, I'd guess, and lately sort of frail and frightened like someone has ruined her forever.

Serena has the face of a high school queen a few beers and speed bumps past her shine, and sharp elbows and tidy breasts that frame a furrowed butterfly tattoo. Her eyes dart around and avoid mine altogether now, but they're still deep lovely blues that could reel anyone in. They must've gotten her into places in life, into blind corners where her choices were made. She's got an against-odds grace that makes me yearn for something that I can't identify — a melancholy like pluvial after desert monsoons. I could fall in love with her.

She talks lots of little things. "I want to put some flowers by the front door," she walks out and says one day as I water my brown front lawn. "What color flowers?"

"Yellow and red would match the trim," I lie, looking over at their duplex and its gray, peeling door and a thick smudge that forms a circle around its knob.

Entire place has a gray and brown pall. Every damn thing in the desert looks gray and brown after awhile.

"Yeah, maybe. That'd be nice," she says, and cuts to: "Cassidy has an ear infection that needs taking care of. I don't know how the hell we're gonna pay for it. Those fucking doctors get all twisted, and the money …"

Serena moves away mid-sentence like something somewhere urgently needs doing. She's wearing a fading blue halter-top, cut-offs and her back is sunburned. She reappears with a laundry basket filled with wet clothes and steps hastily to the clothesline, plastic flip-flops snapping in the hot dust. Raising two children has made her upper body powerful, lithesome but it gives her a slight stoop. With one arm pressing the basket to the sharp edge of her hip she arranges the family garments— shirts, underwear, girl dresses, pants and socks— on the line and clothespins each into place with a hyper-focused precision and rhythm. What would take me 20 minutes to complete she does in less than five.

Mom and Dad go at it usually not long after dinner, just past sunset, Miller Time. Dad scared me at first, appeared greasy and mean, and menace seemed to surround him. He's dark-skinned, Yugoslavian, and the color gives him a shadowy look, even in sunshine. He just looks tough; deep facial lines born of late nights and early rises, hard living, hard work. At 33 he could be 50.

After some months of living across from him we begin to talk. He loves *The Simpsons*. He loves his work. He loves his beer. Cassidy isn't his but he loves her like she is. He beams when he talks of "his girls." He works construction gigs, mostly installs plumbing in new houses. That's his specialty, the plumbing. He's told me dozens of times.

Dad's daily uniform is jeans, work boots and a black or blue t-shirt. Short, messy hair. Weekend days are often spent under the hood of his pickup, a faded milky green rattlebox, where his tools are stored in the back under lock and key.

Sometimes Mom and Dad's arguments spill out the front door onto the gravel drive. I'd lean over my sink and watch through my kitchen window. Mom rushes out first, stumbling on those flip-flops, cheeks wet in porch light. Dad follows closely, two steps behind, a Miller in one hand, hard pointing with the other. Two hoarse and percussive voices out of time with each other rising and falling, his leading about the money and where did it go and did she buy more of the shit? But I've never seen him pop her one. They wear out after about an hour, and peace comes around — a simulation, or maybe a release, of some harmony and some love. A few days later they hit repeat.

———————

After the sirens, Cassidy lifts a thick row of hair from the side of Tiffany's head and gently pulls a brush through it. She carefully straightens the handful of hair, removes a purple hair tie from her mouth and fashions a lopsided pigtail. Tiffany's eyes are closed, and Cassidy's hands feel like Mom's, they tickle, and goosebumps rise on her arms.

This morning Mom cooked breakfast for her husband and daughters, made sure everyone was dressed and ready to go. Dad peeled his pickup out of the gravel driveway and headed for the construction site.

Later, Mom stepped from the apartment alone, carrying her purse.

She looked hollow, cooked on crystal meth. As she moved hastily through her children's gravel-yard salon she said she was "going to the store, be home really soon." Tiffany and Cassidy acknowledged without looking up, continued with the glamour steps.

Mom didn't turn and look back. She rounded out of the driveway with that hasty gait and slight stoop, down the street and out of sight.

The store was the nearby gas station, not even a mile away. Mom walked the shadeless street of skeletal desert trees as the sun burned. Nobody walks outside on a summer day in Tucson, Arizona, not even dogs. The newspaper that night said she entered the cool, convenient environment and said, "number 8." The cashier took the money but didn't notice that there was no car parked at number 8. He said her face was pale.

Then Mom walked casually over to the gas pump. She

pulled the dispenser from its holder and pressed the button for regular unleaded. Trembling, she lifted the dispenser above her head, pointed it down on herself, closed her eyes, and, without pausing for a deep breath, or even a second thought, pulled the lever. Mom showered herself in fuel, all $5 worth. With eyes still closed, she dropped the gas hose to the ground. Witnesses said she fished a lighter from her cutoffs, struggled with its slippery wheel until a spark flashed and she disappeared into flame. She spun in circles, silently, with her arms outstretched — just like her daughters would sometimes do in my yard to get all dizzy.

Soon the sirens arrived.

It's the day after Mom's suicide and there's a knock at my door. I open it to Dad and the girls. He stands there; shirtless, all tanned muscles and tatted biceps, his hard, dark eyes unnaturally swollen. Tiffany rests in his arms; her head pressed against the side of his, arms around his neck, pigtails twisted. Her eyes met mine with zero amazement. Cassidy's at his side, her tanned arms wrapped around him, face pressed against his lower ribs. She holds him tightly as if anchoring him to the ground, as if he might float away somewhere without her. She looks up at me, completely expressionless, with her lovely blue eyes. She doesn't say a word.

Dad stays silent and he looks at me. His torso trembles and he begins to weep. Right there at my front door. He just cries and cries and cries while his entire body shakes.

Tiffany turns her head around and looks out toward the street, a pigtail in Daddy's face. I've never seen a guy like this cry before, not even my old man. I just stand there, useless.

Cassidy looks right at me, expecting nothing.

———————————————

Dad said Mom hadn't slept for the last three nights before she died and had spent all the family's food money on crystal meth.

Cassidy and Tiffany are now living alone with Dad. He doesn't know much about raising girls, about how to dress them for school, or how to braid their hair or wash their clothes. How to talk about their first periods, their first boy.

I can see Cassidy change. I can picture her in some near future, in cutoffs and a Hot Topic shirt, wobbly in her first pair of big-heeled boots, starting to write "hot" and "Pete Wentz" next to boys' pictures in her yearbook. I can see her emerging as some kind of high-school siren guided by a fierce yearning for praise and approval, and then slipping into womanhood by accident. Just like Mom.

Coda Table of Contents

Coca

Playlists

Like most other folks, music fueled life for me, and mainly in lovely ways. It connected me to worlds beyond my grasp, places that bloomed in daydreams, and later became real. If you listen hard enough, things happen. Music also nearly ruined my life a few times. But at a tender age it mostly changed me. It taught me what to read, and how to think, and dream. The dreaming. Before books, and before sadnesses of living set in, there was the music.

So these playlists fit loosely with the stories in this collection mainly because these were the songs I listened to while writing them. Some fit the narrative and the tone—from the punk rock to the wrenching soul ballads. I wanted to share these songs written by others not to enhance the stories, but maybe to use as a kind of soundtrack, away from the book, like emotional bookmarks. Maybe that's bad. But that's how the songs work for me.

Some I listened to crazily, over and over and over, like Dennis Wilson's heartbreaking "Love Remember Me." That song, for example, helped me to withdraw to that place where no one else exists, that same melancholy corner I lived in when I was a kid. It's where all the ghosts are.

For convenience, these playlists are all cued up at Spotify.

"Lost in the Supermarket"

Sweet Suburbia
Skids

Why Can't I Touch It?
Buzzcocks

Synthetic World
Jimmy Cliff

Germ Free Adolescents
X-Ray Spex

Quick as Rainbows
Kitchens of Distinction

Beatles and Stones
The House of Love

Happy People
The Weirdos

Only After Dark
Mick Ronson

The Ballad of Lucy Jordan
Marianne Faithfull

Home is Where the Hatred Is
Esther Phillips

The House Song
Lee Hazlewood

Someone's Coming
The Who

Day After Day
Badfinger

Union City Blue
Blondie

Life From a Window
The Jam

Straight to Hell
The Clash

Smash It Up
The Damned

Lost in the Supermarket
The Clash

"The Grand Prix"

Black Sheep Boy
Tim Hardin

Thirteen
Big Star

I Gotta Getta
The Undertones

Beat Your Heart Out
The Zeros

Soda Pressing
The Boys

Remember the Lightning
20/20

Skyway
The Replacements

My Crazy Afternoon
The Muffs

Tiny Spark
Brendan Benson

Come on, Come on
Cheap Trick

Stay Free
The Clash

Beat Your Heart Out
The Distillers

1 2 3
The Professionals

Shout Above the Noise
Penetration

Dazzle
Siouxsie and the Banshees

Cheap Emotions
Rich Kids

Stay With Me
The Dictators

Never Get Away
The Waldos

Ruby Soho
Rancid

Stay Beautiful
Manic Street Preachers

"Spent Saints"

Fresh as a Daisy
Emitt Rhodes

Someday I Will Treat You Good
Sparklehorse

Calling All Destroyers
TSAR

Wild and Free
Curtis Mayfield

Moonlight Mile
The Rolling Stones

Crayon Angels
Judee Sill

Draft Morning
The Byrds

When You're Near
Ruthann Friedman

Miss Butter's Lament
Harry Nilsson

Topanga Canyon
John Phillips

Be With Me
The Beach Boys

Echoes
Gene Clark

Helter Skelter
The Beatles

Never Learn Not to Love
The Beach Boys

California Earthquake
Mama Cass

Wounded Bird
Graham Nash

Love Remember Me
Dennis Wilson

I Can Hear Music
The Beach Boys

"Eye for Sin"

Red Balloon
Tim Hardin

Don't Let Me Wait Too Long
George Harrison

Bye Bye Pride
The Go-Betweens

La Tristesse Durera (Scream to a Sigh)
Manic Street Preachers

It's All Too Much
The Beatles

You Drive Me Nervous
Alice Cooper

Draw the Line
Aerosmith

TV Tan
The Wildhearts

Ode to a Black Man
The Dirtbombs

When You Walk In the Room
Jackie DeShannon

Gap Toothed Girl
Dan Stuart

Kitty Can
Bee Gees

Fools
The Only Ones

The Stealer
Bettye Lavette

Heart's Delight
Buddy Miles

Run Now
Tommy Keene

Lost Horizons
Gin Blossoms

"No Wheels"

King of California
Dave Alvin

Wash Us Away
Ian Hunter

Speak Now or Forever Hold Your Peace
Terry Reid

Glory
Television

Ask Me No Questions
Johnny Thunders

Just Like Tom Thumb's Blues
Frankie Miller

The Last Chance Texaco
Rickie Lee Jones

Addicted
Jesse Malin

Spanish Stroll
Mink DeVille

Diamonds By the Yard
Elliott Murphy

Hazel Eyes
Redd Kross

I Fell into Painting Houses in Phoenix Arizona
Richmond Fontaine

Even Trolls Love Rock and Roll
Tony Joe White

Have You Seen My Baby?
Randy Newman

April Fool
Patti Smith

I Hear You Calling
Bill Fay

I've Lost Everything I've Ever Loved
David Ruffin

People Ain't No Good
Nick Cave & the Bad Seeds

My Guardian Angel
The Pistoleros

Outtasite (Outta Mind)
Wilco

Phoenix
Aimee Mann

"The Delivery Man"

Silverline
Departure Lounge

Round & Round (It Won't Be Long)
Neil Young

Lost
David Garza

Sweethearts on Parade
M. Ward

Wire and Wheels
Super J Lounge

Runnin' Away
Sly and the Family Stone

How Many Times
Dope Lemon

When the Daylight Comes
Ian Hunter

Novocaine
Alice Cooper

I Don't Want to Grow Up
Ramones

The Return of Jackie and Judy
Ramones

He's Misstra Know-It-All
Stevie Wonder

Rock Steady
Aretha Franklin

Let Forever Be
The Chemical Brothers

Kingdom Come
Tom Verlaine

This Will Be Our Year
The Zombies

Edge of the Universe
Bee Gees

"Grams"

Mama's Boy
Suzi Quatro

Queen Bitch
David Bowie

Ramona
Ramones

Roxy Roller
Nick Gilder

Jupiter Liar
T. Rex

Tomorrow, Wendy
Concrete Blonde

Little Bird
The Beach Boys

Angel of Eighth Ave.
Mott the Hoople

Turn the Tide
Paley Brothers

Mr. Fix-It Man Man
Sisters Love

Crazy Horses
The Osmonds

(Your Love Has Lifted Me) Higher
Esther Phillips

Sitting in Limbo
Jimmy Cliff

Raped and Freezin'
Alice Cooper

I Can Hear the Grass Grow
The Move

Save Me
Smokey Robinson & The Miracles

Mama Roux
Dr. John

Here Come the Nice
Small Faces

Almost With You
The Church

She Ain't Going Nowhere
Guy Clark

"Old Ladies in Church Hats"

Transcendental Blues
Steve Earle

Angels Tonight
Gin Blossoms

Like in the Movies
The Black Watch

The Love I Saw in You Was Just a Mirage
Smokey Robinson & The Miracles

Stronger Than Love
James Carr

Breakfast in Bed
Dusty Springfield

It's Raining Today
Scott Walker

This Is the Thanks I Get
Barbara Lynn

I Don't Care Anymore
Doris Duke

Speed of Sound
Chris Bell

These Days
Ian Matthews

We the People
The Staple Singers

In the Meantime
Betty Davis

All the Good Ones Are Taken
Ian Hunter

"Ghosts and Fireflies"

Straight Line to the Kerb
Departure Lounge

Northern Sky
Nick Drake

Trigger Happy
Lloyd Cole

No Roses Red
Chris Cacavas

If I Needed You
Townes Van Zandt

I Wish It Would Rain
The Temptations

Aretha
The Codgers

See How We Are
X

Acadian Driftwood
The Band

Mississippi
Bob Dylan

Coldest Night of the Year
Vashti Bunyan

Oh Yoko!
John Lennon

All of My Life
Todd Snider

Ends of the Earth
Lord Huron

"Sirens"

Roll on Babe
Ronnie Lane & Slim Chance

Time Wraps Around You
Velvet Crush

Something on Your Mind
Karen Dalton

In the Square
The Pretty Things

On the Way Home
Buffalo Springfield

That's the Way
Led Zeppelin

On & On
Longpigs

Who's Jon
Now It's Overhead

Tucson Kills
Billy Sedlmayr

Music is Love
David Crosby

The Whole of the Moon
The Waterboys

Lorelai
Fleet Foxes

Stewart's Coat
Rickie Lee Jones

May This Be Love
Emmylou Harris

A Conversation with Brian Smith…

I imagine you are very used to seeing your words in print after nearly two decades as a journalist and columnist. In fact, I saw you contributed music essays to two books published earlier this year, but does it feel different to have your very own work of fiction published? How?

It's terrifying. I've written things in the past that had real consequences. Twice I had my life threatened from stories I wrote. One time in Detroit I was punched so hard in the face my eye was swollen shut for days. The guy hated what I wrote, but I'm pretty sure I was just telling the truth. With fiction, it's a different truth, a bigger one (we hope) in that the stories can ultimately define whatever moment we're suffering through, or bouncing through with joy in our steps. That's what my favorite writers, like Dorothy Allison, Bonnie Jo Campbell, Willy Vlautin, Denis Johnson, Jim Harrison, Harry Crews and Charles Bukowski always did or do, somehow. I hope I can do a little of that for someone, somewhere. It's about self-definition, and empathy for the world around us. These things that allow us to breath in and breath out. I'm always terrified I fail at that. So that's what's scary.

A lot of these stories take us to harrowing physical and emotional spaces. How much of this book is based on seeds of truth?

Well it is memoirish in some ways. I mean, I was strung out on meth and alcohol. The latter for years and years. I played in rock 'n' roll bands that developed sizable followings and we made albums and toured. And I worked with rock 'n' roll stars and gifted producers, and so on. I also worked as a journalist in Phoenix and Detroit, and I've lived on King Cobra in ghettos. I was an obsessed bicycle racer on the U.S. National Team when I was a teen. So themes and characters in the book relate to experiences I've had. It would be absolutely impossible to write about meth and booze addiction if I hadn't lived it.

The hero, Julian, seems particularly taken with the faded glory of Detroit. What was it like to live there just as the city was beginning to be revived?

There are a few lines in the book about how Detroit is the most god-forsaken failure of a once-great American industrial giant. And it's true. It's a city that was once called Paris of the West and then turned into absolute ruin. You can taste the desolation, of abandoned houses and crumbling factories, so you're actually breathing into your lungs the city of Detroit, and sometimes coughing it up. It gets into your system. People walk around with that sense of failure inside of them. And that sense spreads out to the moneyed, mostly white suburbs.

The revival is kind of vile. A few rich white people have bought up the downtown, and for the most part, the revival people talk of is because white people have moved into certain neighborhoods. But Detroit, even in its most desolate, has so much beauty, so much multi-ethnic culture. It kills me to see any of that displaced by white culture. I bought a house in an old, all-black neighborhood and I just fell in love with the people. I was the only white guy for miles. My neighbors were so kind, so gentle. Retired educators, young families, and several who lived on my street for a couple generations. When I moved in, neighbors brought me plants, and fresh baked cookies and even blankets because they thought I might get cold in the winter.

White people were moving and actually calling Detroit "a blank slate." So wrong, and so offensive.

You were once a world-class bike racer, with teammates who went on to the Olympics and the Tour de France. What was it like to suddenly change paths after so much disciplined training?

Well, when I was a teenager and I lived and breathed cycling, it was all I did, and it was one reason why I quit high school at the beginning of 10th grade. I'd go for hard, 80-mile training rides before 8th grade homeroom class. I quit cycling – by then I was pretty much living at the Olympic Training Center in Colorado Springs — when I discovered punk rock, and girls. I was winning races against men much older than me, in way over my head. Later, I watched my old teammate win the gold in Olympic road race while I was drunk on Colt 45, living in a downtown L.A. hell hole with my band members and roadies, just starving and miserable. I had a doctor once tell me that by the time I was 12 I was an addict, because I trained so hard I was actually addicted to endorphins, so when I stopped racing bicycles, I had to replace that high. Alcohol and cocaine became my new way of living, and dealing with depression. I never got into heroin, miraculously. But the crystal meth was much worse.

Much of this book centers on the alcoholism and crystal meth addiction of the central character, Julian. You have been very open as a writer about your own struggles with addiction. What was it like to remember and revisit those days with such painstaking candor?

Honestly it made me want to get high and drunk again, and often. And I'm saying that as a person who nearly died from drinking. When I kicked alcohol for good, it was so scary and horrible I swore I'd never ever suffer like that again. I should've been in a hospital. I'm sober. Been that way for years.

Still, I crave alcohol (beer, mostly) often, and cocaine and meth sometimes. I hear that little voice say how those wicked jolts would allow me to feel normal again.

It's those little gifts that keep on giving, I'm telling ya.

I know that on your upcoming national book tour you will be reading not just at independent bookshops, but also record stores, art house theaters and sober houses. What kind of venue are you most looking forward to and why?

I grew up in record stores, and, a little later, book stores. Those stores are still my favorite places to go in any city, they smell like my living room and music room. Other than strolling the backstreets and non-corporatized areas on foot, those few stores that remain are the best way to get a feel for any town. At least for me. I got a lot of my early music education from record store employees, who I thought as a kid were real rock stars. They knew all about The Buzzcocks and The Ramones and The Clash, the stuff I loved.

I never read books in school, rarely went to school. There weren't very many times when I could afford books, so I'd go and hang at a store and read at the library. I learned how to write from reading and from working in journalism with really gifted editors. Never went to a writing class or workshop – was always too frightened. So yes, record and book stores, my living rooms. But also sober houses.

I didn't write these stories with any underlying message of sobriety, or any of that. But a few people who've read them say addicts like me might get a lot out of them. That's really something. If I can help one meth addict, because I know how absolutely necessary that drug is when you need it to make you happy, to make you normal, and how quickly it devastates, because it did me. It would be an absolute privilege to read at a sober house.

Much like the main character, you actually fronted not just one but several rock bands. Are you ever tempted to return to performing? Will this tour see you sing and read from *Spent Saints*?

No singing. I spent years fronting rock 'n' roll bands. I lived and breathed that, and I have knee and back injuries and liver damage to prove it. We all figured we'd be dead by 30. And then when we hit 30, we figured we'd all be dead at 35. My then-heroes had all died off fairly young, from Arthur Rimbaud to Johnny Thunders. I really believed the shit was going to finish me off, if the depression didn't. Along the way I learned to write songs too, and survived for a short while on that. I drank and played music and had great loves and read books and wrote songs. That was my life, and it sounds pretty sweet. But for me the drinking became the most important thing, and the drugs, and, of course, the attendant sadnesses and ugliness that go with that stuff. I learn most everything important and sustaining in life from women, always have since I was a child, and then even that couldn't save me. Not at all. Ultimately I think I stopped playing music unconsciously because it became hard for me to do it sober. I lived for years waking up and wishing I could die. Sounds awful and selfish, and it is. And it's no way to live. But somehow I needed to live. It's a struggle for me everyday, still. I remind myself daily that life exists in all the small wonders. As corny as it sounds, I know I'm OK if a desert sunset can move me to tears, one all scraped up by power lines and mesquite trees.

Ten different up and coming directors have contributed their own unique visions to bring *Spent Saints* to life. What is it like watching versions of your stories on the big screen? Did you ever think your writing would inspire a cartoon? Or a contemporary dance?

You kidding? No, not at all, not in a million years. These beautiful films and movements, and the interest from the people creating them, absolutely blows my mind. It's already crazy flattering that these super-skilled directors like the stories. But then they like them enough to translate them into mini-films? And for no money. It's absolutely life-affirming. And the interpretations are interesting, to see what they pick up on, the nuances, particularly the sped-up horror of crystal meth — and that nervous system damage — interpreted in graceful dance. These two worlds collide. It's brilliant and also very moving. Mostly I think everything I write is worthless and nobody will like any of it, and then this sort of thing happens. These people are finding meanings.

The very intimate first-person narration is both compelling and cinematic. Do you see this book being turned into a television series or a feature film? Is that something you had in mind while writing it?

No. That's so pretentious sounding. Equally pretentious to say that I was feeling all suicidal too. But I was. I really just had to write. I got laid off my writing gig at a Detroit newspaper and I had nothing. There was a woman, of course, who kept on me to write.

One of the stories, "Ghosts and Fireflies", focuses on depression and suicide. What would you say to readers who relate to your character in this way? Where and how should they begin to seek help?

Hmm. I sought help because I wanted to off myself. Look, I have a few very close friends who did just that and it always made sense to me. I get it, man. I just couldn't seem to exist in a world that felt like it was designed for other people. Nothing against anyone else, it just wasn't for me. That feeling is the ultimate in isolation because there's no relief. I'd be in a room full of people I love and the depressing afternoon light always carried in its ray of weighty hopelessness, and it'd be slanting in through dirty windows, and that would be all I could focus on. And this was a time in my life when everything else was good. I had a love and a nice place to live, writing work, and food to eat.

I think if you're laying out plans to kill yourself you should probably seek help. But that's the last thing anyone does when the desperation is absolutely exasperating.

If you could look back and give your teenaged self any one piece of advice, what would it be?

Drink less, write more.

So many debut authors are MFA graduates these days, yet you never finished high school. Can you speak for a minute about being an award-winning writer with limited formal education? Has being an autodidact given you an edge?

I don't know if there's any edge from being self-taught. I tell myself there is. I will say the fact I didn't go to school for writing instilled in me a complete sense of inferiority over the years. I got my first full-time writing gig when I was still drinking and doing drugs. To my left was a Harvard grad, and to my right a Columbia grad, and me, an alcoholic high school dropout in the middle. It was downright comical, but scary too.

But I have found myself in countless situations that I otherwise would've missed out on had I gone to college and then an MFA program. From life-threatening (like, say, kicking alcohol or having guns pulled on me) to what-the-fuck-am-I doing-here incredible (I've found myself in wretched meth labs surrounded by porn and filthy kids in diapers, and also on stage with my band in front of 10,000 people).

I always get super nervous reading stories to rooms filled with MFAs and writing professors, but every time I do I seem to win them over. I've given talks in University classrooms about writing and journalism, and used myself as an example of what not to do when pursuing a career in writing or journalism. A few of my favorite contemporary writers came out of MFA programs, and many others did not, and those who are strictly autodidactic really inspire me.

What is the next project you are working on? When can we expect to see it in print or onscreen?

I'm working on a novel featuring Julian from *Spent Saints*. Hopefully a movie based on the script I wrote about Doug Hopkins, my friend who committed suicide, after he wrote hit songs for the Gin Blossoms. Some other things. I'm continuing to write a column in the Tucson Weekly called Tucson Salvage, and it's mostly about people I meet who live in the fringes, or are overlooked in some way; folks who define that city for me. There's talk of those columns coming out in a book.

Acknowledgments

Mi padre, mi héroe: Howard M. Smith (RIP)

La Familia: Mom Mary (RIP), Lois, Barry, Marcia, Stuart, Julie, Travis, Tulah, Blake, Paul, Eddie, Moose, John S., John G., Teresa, Don, Dave and Barb, and the Herrlings.

Todos mis editores que me enseñaron todo lo: Jeremy Voas, W. Kim Heron, Kate Nolan, Gil Garcia, Bob Mehr, Mari Herreras, Eric Waggoner.

Editor de mi libro: John "Cal" Freeman.

Desde mi corazón: Maggie Rawling, Cybelle Codish, Robin Johnson, Michael Brooks and Keith Jackson and all my Beat Angel brothers, Eddie Baranek, Richard C. Rollins, Dr. Rafeal Gonzalez (RIP), Patrick Scott O'Connor, Douglas Hopkins (RIP), Amy Silverman, Shireen Liane, Jonathan Daniel, Gilby Clarke, Nate Cavalieri, Peter Gilstrap, Billy Sedlmayr, Alan "Box" Fischer, Super J Lounge, Chandra Porto, Laurie Notaro, Clif Taylor, Vincent Sprague, Jason Schusterbauer, Mike Joyce, Taver Resetar, Joel Martin, Dennis Rhodes.

Por creer en mí: M.L. Liebler and Ridgeway Press.

Brian Smith has written for many magazines and alt-weeklies, and his fiction has appeared in a variety of literary journals. He's an award-winning journalist, first as a staff writer and columnist at Phoenix *New Times* and then as an editor at Detroit's *Metro Times*. Before writing full time, Smith was a songwriter who fronted rock 'n' roll bands Beat Angels and, before that, GAD. He has penned tunes with lots of folks, including Alice Cooper. At one point he overcame heady crystal meth and alcohol addictions. As a kid growing up in Tucson, Ariz., Smith was a national class bicycle racer. He now lives back in Tucson where he writes a regular column in the *Tucson Weekly* centered on unsung heroes, people on the fringes and the desolate beauty found in unlikely places. *Spent Saints* is his debut collection of short stories.

243